KATIE DID

by Sheryl Pascal Gormley

This book, like my other, is dedicated to my kids.
They know my love of the written word
and urge me to write and be happy.

I'm also indebted to fellow writers at
Ormond Writers' League who, through their
critique, encourage me forward.

CHAPTER ONE

Although Katie wondered what time it was, she hesitated to look at her watch. Just a peek at the long, narrow, barred window and she'd know if daylight had begun. Instead, she flopped over facedown on the uncomfortable metal cot. The routine noises, that annoyed her at first, now made little impact by their presence. As she tried to block out all sights and sounds she buried her head in her folded arms.

Her ears caught the sound of rain as it hammered outside against the dull, gray walls. Again. *My god, will it ever stop? Seems like it's been raining for a year.* She squeezed her eyes shut, as if that would erase the pounding that, by now, she felt inside. Gloom penetrated her soul. A rumbling of thunder in the distance now and then didn't help.

With all her heart she wished she could cry and rid herself of built-up despair and anger. As the deluge continued she decided, that since she had no tears left, the sky was taking over and pouring out its sadness for her. A sweeping chill caused a shudder. She burrowed deeper beneath the threadbare cover. She drew her knees to her chest, wrapped her arms around her legs and curled into a fetal position. No moisture escaped her eyes. It collected within. Surely the time would come that she'd break loose and drown in her own tears.

Although Katie was not quite certain she wanted it to be morning, from the sounds that filtered through, she knew it must be. A night of fitful sleep left her disoriented. Random thoughts bounced around in her head and wouldn't fit together properly. *Who am I? Where am I?* Then. quite out of character, *aah, who the hell cares anyway?*

Her brain took a while to shift into position. Why was she having such trouble remembering? She'd certainly been here long enough. Hurray. She was in jail. And cold. Shivering head to toe. *Has the boiler room screwed up again?* One could never depend on having a comfortable temperature level in this ancient place. No matter the time of year it was maintained with an as-we-feel-like-it attitude.

With the city's growth and expansion the jail, originally ten miles past the outskirts, was now located at the edge of the business district. The concrete block building was a sprawling, U-shaped, ten-story structure ugly to look at from inside or out. Lack of windows was apparent. The top four levels, however, displayed a regular series of tall, narrow openings. From the ground it wasn't obvious, but they were windows and each contained a row of bars. The vertical bars were placed such a distance apart that no one could squeeze between them in the unlikely event the Plexiglas might be shattered by human force.

The open end of the U housed a small dirt area, commonly called 'the little yard'. Over the years the name shortened to the acronym, LILY. It was enclosed with a high chain link fence topped with coiled barbed wire. The guards had the nerve to call it an athletic field.

This was jail, not a high-security prison. A person found guilty of a violent crime would be here only until the trial was over. If found guilty, they'd be sent somewhere else to serve the sentence. Still, it was not inconceivable someone might try to escape.

Most of the small offices filling the first two floors of the building were cramped and cluttered with stacks of manila folders bulging with papers. Cobwebs, gracing many corners, were the only artwork. A desk sandwiched between two straight wooden chairs, a file cabinet and a bookcase, the only furnishing in each. Additional chairs could be found scattered in the hall should there be a need for them. These rooms were rented by lawyers and bail bondsmen.

Floors three through five were courtrooms, the only decent-looking rooms in the entire building. True to tradition, the walls of each were finished with luxurious mahogany paneling. Judge's bench, jury box, and all other furniture and accessories were of matching wood and polished brass trim. As intended, those entering the room were impressed and respectful of the implication of the décor. Those on trial felt extra emotions: they were anxious and intimidated by the same scene as they were brought before the court.

* * *

The morning sounds seldom varied. Inmates carried on their regular noisy conversations. Some swore it was much later than usual and demanded the guards take them to the cafeteria for breakfast *now*. Some covertly threatened other inmates, still others tried to complete a trade of personal stash: two sticks of gum for a cigarette.

In the months she'd been here snow had fallen several times. Bitterly cold outside, temperatures often hovered barely above zero. The wind chill factor made it treacherous to spend any time outside in the LILY. The dirt yard was still frozen solid but at last with some help from the rain, the few remaining clumps of ugly, filthy snow were melting away.

Inside was at least dry, but with the furnace being so temperamental it was seldom warm. Katie reconsidered and decided that it wasn't lack of heat that produced the chill—her nerves were on edge. That's what created the discomfort.

She swung her bare feet over the side of the cot and stood. With both hands on her forehead she pushed her fingers back through her thick brown hair. The unruly strands were pulled up and held in place with an elastic band, soon hidden by the curls. If you didn't know, it would be difficult to tell whether it was styled into a ponytail, or just cut short. Drawing her hands down over her face again she rubbed her eyes. The remnants of sleep were hard to erase.

Katie reached under the cot and dug out the fleece-lined slipper-style footwear. It seemed her feet could never get warm enough. When winter made life more miserable, Susan, her best friend, visited more often and had brought the slippers for Katie. Now she slid her feet into them and wiggled her toes. They'd help keep contact with the cold, hard floor at a minimum. It was a thoughtful gift and she appreciated it. Katie paced in circles urging her blood to circulate, to clear her head, and organize her thoughts as another the day began.

A few cells away Livia's radio was tuned to a Golden Oldies station and blared Santana's *Black Magic Woman*. " Don't turn your back on me, baby, " Livia sang right along with it as if she believed *she* was the black magic woman. No matter what, Livia always seemed to be happy. "I got myself in here, honey," s he'd said. "And I'll damn well get myself out. Might as well be happy when I can."

Katie had kept a relatively level head in the beginning, but never got to the 'place' Livia was in. In fact, she envied it a little and wished she were able to figure out how to adjust her own thoughts and make the best out of her miserable situation.

Under the narrow window Katie stood on the edge of her cot, balancing carefully. As she peered toward sky the color of slate and than looked down, a thin slice of the outside world fell into her line of vision. In the heavy, dismal morning a traditional late-winter picture emerged.

From the distance she watched dozens of people as they scurried about. Most headed in the same direction, looking like ants bringing supplies to the hill. Moving at more than their normal rate of speed many ran to protect themselves from the bitter weather. Umbrellas, bouncing dots of color diffused by the rain, offered little protection to those who attempted to keep the wind from turning them inside out. Long, dark coattails flapped against swirling raindrops.

Uncontrollably, another quick shiver raised goose bumps along both Katie's arms. They tried to crawl up her neck as well, but without success—she rubbed them away. Now aware that it was morning rush hour, she estimated the time to be around eight o'clock. The hustle-bustle to get to work by nine. She remembered those not-so-long-ago days.

Yet another quiver ran through her body stealing her breath for a moment. Her hands trembled. She almost lost her grasp on the thin ledge of the window. At last, allowing herself to mentally step into reality, it came back to her. The whole ugly event seeped into her thoughts. Her conscious mind was shocked into gear.

Yes, it was stormy outside. Certainly cold. But the chills she experienced had nothing at all to do with the weather. For all intents and purposes winter was over. This was the end of March and the wind and rain were simply part of it. *It might not be as nasty out there as it looks. You know, that "in like a lamb, out like a lion" thing they say. Spring is right around the corner.*

Of course, there might be a malfunction in the boiler room, but if the temperature hovered at eighty degrees she'd still be shivering. The significant thing was that the time had come. Today would be The Day. She felt it. And Wilsky's 'rumor' supported what Katie's intuition told her.

Her life, the life of Katie Hagen or what was left of it, would be decided by total strangers. There were only two choices: guilty of murder in the first degree, or, not guilty.

The twelve men and women of the jury had been given instructions three days ago and deliberations had continued almost non-stop since then.

Matron Janetta Wilsky had paused at Katie's cell as she was doing this morning's check. "Hey, Katie, I've got a rumor to pass on to you."

"Okay, Wilsky, what's the joke this time?" Katie asked. She was cranky, and more nervous than she'd been the entire time. The jury was out and, surely, this ordeal would end soon. Maybe in the next few hours. She was in no mood to listen to Wilsky feed her some joke or riddle. Not now. Save it for some other time. At this moment she had too much on her mind to pay attention to any of that stuff.

"Hey, grouch, your loss," Wilsky said, and made a move to turn and walk away. She liked Katie, and glanced back to check the temperament of one or her favorite inmates. She knew how difficult the last few weeks had been on her. The last couple of days especially. In a different time and place she and Katie might have become close friends.

"Sorry," said Katie, immediately apologetic. She remembered that, although rough and tough, Wilsky had a warm side that she didn't hesitate to show. She treated all the inmates with respect. "I'm really stretched thin with all that's been going on lately." Katie forced a weak smile.

"I know, I know," Wilsky said, nodding. "Well, I'm not joking with you today, and it is truly a rumor, but it sort of looks like the jury may be about ready to announce. They've already asked for their breakfast, and yesterday or the day before it wasn't delivered to them anything close to this early. Something's going on. I just don't know what."

Katie sucked in her breath and felt so lightheaded she slumped down on her cot. So maybe it would be this morning. *Of course it's nothing more than a rumor. Maybe they only wanted a piece of testimony cleared up or an article of law clarified. Juries often do that prior to handing down the verdict. But, word sometimes travels through strange channels. So, today?*

Verdict. The word landed like a bomb ready to explode in Katie's head. Well, at least it would be over. One way or the other she'd have some sort of relief.

"I almost wish you hadn't said anything." Katie said.

"Can't take it back, now," said Wilsky. " But I thought you'd like to know. I suppose it's not quite Kosher for me to be saying anything to you, but rumors do fly, don't they? "

During the past months the two women had many personal chats. Wilsky felt Katie should not spend the rest of her life behind bars, no matter what they said she'd done. The prosecution asked for the death penalty but everyone knew, even if they found her guilty, she would remain in jail for years before that happened. No, not jail. Prison would be her next residence. From what she's heard and read, a much more brutal place to be than a county jailhouse.

"Well, of course you're right. I'd rather know. This waiting around can drive a person nuts," said Katie. "Thanks, Wilsky."

"Yeah, kiddo. And good luck. Really, really good luck to you." She patted the metal bars of the door. Katie watched Wilsky as she turned to continue the morning check. Wilsky's slender, muscular, body encased in chocolate brown slacks and crisp tan shirt, seemed more powerful today than usual. *Maybe it's not the body that seems powerful all of a sudden, maybe it's those words that swing the weight.*

Luck. As if she were off to a tennis match. Or a dental appointment. Luck, indeed! Well, Katie couldn't totally ignore that. It was a factor she'd be depending on heavily the next few hours. Correction: *good* luck. Keep those fingers crossed. Her vision blurred temporarily. Her stomach churned. Aware that she might vomit, she swallowed rapidly to keep it down.

Until now so much of this ordeal seemed like a bad dream. Or maybe like something she was watching on television. Nothing she was part of. This was none of those. Reality jumped out at her, big and bold.

CHAPTER TWO

From the first day, Katie had been surprised by Wilsky's attitude. Not what she expected at all. Books, television and movies portrayed a law-enforcement matron as some big, ox-like broad void of anything resembling humanity. A rough, tough, bitchy woman issuing orders, making demands. One whose only communication snapped out in curt monosyllables. Wilsky didn't fit any part of that description. With no hesitation Katie realized that Janetta Wilsky was an intelligent woman, who treated those under her watch fairly. A far cry from the horror stories.

When problems arose, as they inevitably did on occasion, Wilsky handled the situation swiftly and with a competence and instinct that never failed to floor newcomers. This impressed Katie. She began to feel she had, if not a friend, at least an ally.

Katie and Wilsky quickly developed a rapport. Though no special favors were granted, many conversations between the two were as pleasant as could be expected under the circumstances. Often, they spent part of an afternoon talking quietly, delving into each other's lives and how each came to be at this location.

"Wilsky," Katie once asked, "why in the world would you want to be a warden or matron or whatever it is that's your title?"

"Well," Wilsky replied, "at one point in my life I'd planned for a career in journalism. I was still in college and not close to being professional, of course. I was a young idealistic female always thinking how the world *should* be. On my own, I decided to write a piece about a woman's jail or prison. I had no idea at all of the realities, so I made several calls. I scheduled visits to a couple of jails. Based on my journalistic skills I asked to interview a few employees." She paused, thinking back some fifteen years.

"That was all it took?" asked Katie.

"No. Well, actually yes, I guess. When I saw the horrible conditions these women lived in, and knew they had no hope, I thought I could make a difference. So many of them didn't care one way or the other about their own life. More often than not, the facility personnel also showed complete indifference.

"Seemed to me that something, however small, could be done to change an atrocious situation into one that was at least close to tolerable. So I added a class to my college workload: Women in the Criminal Justice System. Later I took Criminal Justice Administration. So I'm still hoping to make a difference. How many times have you heard a story like that?"

"Do you *like* it? Has it been worth all the crap you have to take from the inmates and the higher-ups?" asked Katie. "Why do you think these awful people deserve anything at all? They put themselves here. I have zero sympathy for any of them. Even myself. I was more stupid than I thought possible. And gullible. We all pretty much deserve what we get. This isn't supposed to be a vacation, you know. It's punishment."

"You know, Katie, I don't think I could handle a real prison. The kind that handles violent criminals. A lot of those are some truly nasty ladies. Many of them are lifers. Here, I am not exposed to those with big time charges, murderers and so forth. Most of what I see is low-life drug dealers, petty theft, and prostitutes who have gone a bit too far with their businesses. Not many will be here long. And most will return. It's sad. A bit of a break here and there must help, don't you think?

"Here, with the milder side of the ugly, if a situation looks as though it might get out of control I'll call in help. I have no interest in being a hot dog. Even in this place you can get hurt."

"No murderers, eh?" asked Katie. "What do you think I'm here for?"

"Oops, sorry," said Wilsky. "Somehow you don't strike me as a murderer."

"Yeah, well, you can't judge a book by its cover can you?"

Wilsky cocked her head to one side and studied Katie for a moment, trying to determine whether she was serious or just being sarcastic in order to cover up real feelings. She'd caught Katie doing that now and then, and felt sure Katie had no idea how transparent she appeared when trying to play the tough guy.

Deciding to change the subject she said, "Feel like going to the gym for a workout today? I can get you the time, I think. Last time I looked nobody had even signed up, so if you are interested I'll put your name down."

"Sure," said Katie, "it's not like I'll be going anywhere else for a while. And if I don't work at it, this body will be a marshmallow soon. Now that I've started a regular routine I'd damn well better keep it up."

"It's tough for me to set time aside to do that," said Wilsky. "It's not easy like it used to be. Years are creeping up on me, you know, and I need to stay in shape so I can have a little job security."

"They'll never let you get away from here," said Katie. "Don't you know that? You're much too smart. You're valuable. What would they do without you?"

"Yeah, I know," said Wilsky. Then put her hand over her mouth and added, "But you know I'm forty-something, and the older you get the harder it is to stay dedicated. I really have to work at it. I guess it's not all physical skills that keep me here, though." When she said 'forty-something', it might have sounded like 'thirty-something' if you weren't listening closely, but her eyes twinkled and gave her away.

"Nearly everyone respects you. They may not like what you *do,* but they all know that in this job you *have* to do some things. And, hey, lady," teased Katie, "I heard that age thing. Can't fool me. But it does look like you need to talk to Clairol pretty soon. I see a...um, 'distinguished', gray sprinkle in those dark locks!"

Wilsky chuckled and said, "I'll let you know the gym time so you can get that off that soft butt and give your blood a chance to get up to your brain so you can think more clearly." She moved on down the row.

CHAPTER THREE

It was a Wednesday afternoon and many of the cells were empty. Half-a-dozen hookers had been bailed out. They'd be really careful for a few days, maybe even as long as a month. But they'd be accepting lodging here again in the near future. An unending pattern.

Katie had been allowed library time and was in her cell reading when Wilsky walked around doing a body check. The natives were quiet so she stopped to visit with Katie.

"It's your turn today," Wilsky said. "What was your life like? What happened when you were a little girl?"

"Not much," said Katie. "My parents were career people and I sorta came along at a bad time. My mother had a couple of miscarriages early on and thought that was it. So when I popped out I was just in their way. Mother was forty-two years old, daddy nearly fifty, and they loved to travel. Often. Business and pleasure both. Can't do much of that with a baby on your hip.

"I had a nanny for a while and I learned to play alone a lot. It was okay. I resented it for years when I was a little older, but what the hell, they didn't know any better. They knew business, not babies. I'm over it."

"What did you do for fun?" asked Wilsky.

"I played football and basketball and baseball with the boys. There weren't any girls in my neighborhood and I wasn't much into playing dolls anyway."

"So," said Wilsky, "you were a tomboy?"

"Completely," said Katie. "I loved sports and I played as well as a lot of the boys. Better than some." She smiled with satisfaction remembering some childhood achievement.

"Did you ever break a bone?"

"Nah, I was pretty tough," said Katie. "I could take care of myself and didn't scare easily, either. That came much later."

"What about school?"

"I was lucky enough to learn to read when I was really little. Before I started school. One nanny read to me every afternoon and taught me how to read as well. I still love books. Doesn't matter much what the subject is. There's just so much to learn. I want to know as much as my brain can hold. Sometimes I've got two or three books going at the same time."

"Yeah, I've seen you in there almost eating the pages," said Wilsky.

"Beats that stuff on a tray you guys call food," Katie joked. And then, "Looking back, I realize I probably put too much pressure on myself. Everything had to be just perfect. I practiced penmanship till my hand ached. I wanted it to look like it had been done by a machine, I guess. I don't really know. Homework assignments were always finished on time, and," she chuckled, "was teacher's pet more than once. I had a lot more fun at school than I did at home."

As Wilsky listened, she appreciated Katie's conversation. A rare occurrence in this jail. The vast majority of these women were pitifully uneducated. Many had not gone beyond the eighth or ninth grade and had difficulty speaking a complete sentence. Some never made it that far and could barely write their name. Their general attitude was one of resentment. The majority were sullen and uncooperative. Some just apathetic. Katie's wit and Wilsky's own sense of humor brightened up many otherwise monotonous hours for the two of them.

The days, in large part, ran together. There were a few planned events to help alleviate the boredom that prevailed, but those who participated did so half-heartedly. Most simply waited out their time as they formed a plan to go back to their friends on the outside. A more careful plan than before. A smart plan to keep them from returning to this place.

However, once a good behavior pattern had been established, privileges were given that were withheld from habitual troublemakers. The library, inadequately stocked, true, was nonetheless available. Wilsky, in her years there, had taken effective steps to institute various rehabilitation centers that offered instruction in assorted useful crafts and skills. She harbored the hope that it would lead some of the women into productive channels when they returned to life on the outside. If there were only a handful that repaired their broken lives Wilsky could consider the program to have been a success.

Katie used the library regularly, reading several novels more than once, just for entertainment. Textbooks were available and she took advantage of them, too. The more she learned, the better. Besides, knowledge gleaned from studying some legal tomes just might be helpful…on an appeal.

CHAPTER FOUR

Now, with Wilsky, Katie opened up when she talked about her own childhood. It brought back memories that she was not always eager to think about, but a lot she wanted to be sure to remember as well. Elementary school was the beginning of her understanding the value of an education and of being and having a friend. During the first few grades she kept mostly to herelf, but even so had several friends. Mentally traveling back in time, she thought about fourth grade and of her best friend, Susan Wilson.

Katie was an only child. Her friend Susan was the second youngest of seven children. Susan's father was frequently out of work because of a drinking problem that everyone knew of but few talked about. The fact that a constant shortage of money existed in her large family was common knowledge. Although Susan could accept it, many of her classmates couldn't. Kids can be cruel and they often taunted her about her clothes, her family, her house, or whatever they chose at the moment. It was obvious Susan was vulnerable.

One Thursday, in the lunchroom, Alice Carson, the school bully, started bad-mouthing Susan.

"I see ya got peanut butter and jelly again," said Alice. As she spoke her lip curled in a sneer exposing teeth yellowed with mustard from her own ham and cheese sandwich.

"I like it." replied Susan.

"Good thing. Ya had it every day for the last two months." Alice laughed. She looked around the table for approval from the others. Heads turned away.

Susan refused to comment. It was true. Besides, she didn't want to get into any battle with Alice. One always came up a loser against her. Alice, being bigger and a year older than others in her class, had quite a reputation for being mean and hateful. Rumor was that she'd often duked it out with boys to a successful ending. Most students avoided her. They knew she was a snotty kid who went out of her way to pick an argument or a fight. She seldom fought fairly and, unfortunately for the opposition, Alice won a lot more than she lost. Her way of intimidating a person left at least half the kids at school wary of her. It was a well-deserved reputation.

"Do ya have it for dinner, too?" questioned Alice.

Susan's eyes began to fill. With her head down, she sat silent, nibbling on the remains of the sandwich she clutched with both hands. As a sniffle began she put the crust on a napkin and folded her hands on her lap. Willing herself not to cry, she stared down at the table and prayed the tears wouldn't leak out in spite of her efforts.

"Does Daddy have P B & J with his beer? Huh? Or maybe you *have* to have it just so he can *buy* his beer?" Alice was on a roll. No stopping her now. She'd found an easy target and enjoyed it to the hilt. Several other kids quit eating. A nervous hum floated through the air at what was going on, but no one spoke up. Katie sat next to Susan and listened, watching Alice intently. The searing remarks continued.

"Alice, " Katie said quietly across the table. "Cut it out."

Alice didn't stop. This was fun! She chanted her little rhyme: "P B & J, every day; P B & J, every day".

Katie slid her chair back from the cafeteria table and stood. She walked around to the other side where Alice sat. Katie, her eyes filled with fury, bent down close to Alice's ear and, matter-of-factly said, "Lay off her or I'll put your lights out." She turned and walked away.

"Katie!" screeched Susan.

Katie whirled around just in time to be on the receiving end of an open carton of milk thrown at her. As Alice sat there, a nasty, satisfied smile spread across her face. She watched, as the carton, right on target, smacked against Katie's chest sending milk splattering across her clothes and onto the floor.

Using control beyond her years, Katie stood solid as a rock and stared at Alice until at last Alice let her gaze drop and returned to her own lunch, mumbling "Guess I showed her!"

Katie left the lunchroom and found her teacher. Without offering an explanation, she asked for, and was granted, permission to be excused from school for the remainder of the day because her clothes were such a mess.

Katie did not forget the hatefulness against her friend.

Alice did not forget Katie.

I'm gonna get even with her. I absolutely will not take that shit. That damn Katie embarrassed me. In front of everyone. Made me look the fool, even if it was temporary. It's time to pick it up again. Time to let Katie, and, by god, the whole school, know that I'm the strong one. I'm the one to respect. But I'll have to be careful. Let a little time pass. I don't need any more trouble with the teachers!

A few weeks went by. It was Katie's turn to help rearrange the class bulletin board for the new month. Alice waited for the afternoon she knew Katie was scheduled to stay after school. She'd take care of business then.

CHAPTER FIVE

Many of the students, including Katie, used a pathway through a little wooded park nearby, as a shortcut to and from school. Today, however, Katie's nanny drove to pick her up. They had shopping to attend to. So she did not appear at the path at all.

Alice sat fuming as she hid behind the shrubs for half an hour and waited to ambush Katie. Finally, realizing her plan had been sabotaged she trudged on to her own house muttering to herself. Her resolve deepened. Once again she checked schedules looking for the best time to make new plans for the beating she felt Katie deserved. She was anxious to give it to her.

Alice spent a tense two weeks, consumed with revenge, Another opportunity presented itself: the teacher asked Katie to stay after school to assist with a special project. That meant Katie would be leaving school later than the other kids. And she'd travel the path alone.

As she expected Katie to pass by, Alice set her trap. She stayed out of sight behind protection of the bushes. She didn't need to wait long. Katie appeared in view, her arms full of books. She walked leisurely along the pathway toward Alice's hiding place. As Katie neared, Alice held her breath fearful of making the slightest sound and being discovered. She mustn't ruin her plan. She allowed Katie to barely pass by, then leapt from the shrubs and grabbed her from behind. She dragged her to the ground. Books and papers flew in all directions.

Katie squealed as she went down. A couple of seconds passed before Katie realized who was beating on her and why. She had been caught off-guard. Protecting herself now became her only thought. Attempts to fight back were in vain. Alice showed no mercy. She smashed with her fist anywhere she could make contact. She pulled Katie's hair and kicked out when Katie showed any sign of retaliation.

At last Katie managed to break loose. She regained her balance, but as she backed up, she stumbled. Alice lunged at her again, swinging wildly with both arms. Katie pushed at Alice and made her stagger for a moment. Katie took the opportunity to run but tripped and nearly fell to the ground again. Her elbows and knees were already scraped and bloody. The button had popped off her skirt, and the back of her hand was bleeding where Alice had gouged it with her fingernails. Katie maintained her position and gasped for breath. She warily eyed Alice in an effort to calculate her next move.

There was no need for words. They both knew the reason for this. Alice was out to get Katie. Katie decided she wouldn't be got.

Alice went for her again. Katie brought up her knee and used both fists to punch Alice in the stomach dropping her to the ground. Katie seized the opportunity to grab a thin branch from a nearby willow tree and, ripping it through her closed fist, stripped the leaves from it leaving a formidable switch.

Alice wobbled to her feet again. Katie brandished the switch like a bullwhip. She slashed Alice's bare legs, her arms. Each blow stung and made Alice wince and cry out. Alice grabbed for the switch. Katie jerked it back out of her reach and swung it across her face. Alice's hands flew up to protect her eyes.

Now, to the astonishment of both girls, Katie had the advantage. Katie swung rapidly, scoring over and over. Alice fairly danced in an attempt to avoid the punishment from Katie's weapon. Both felt exhausted and out of breath. They hurt all over. Their clothes were dirty and ragged. Neither would give.

Panting, yet leaning toward Alice and holding the switch poised and ready for another attack, Katie whispered, "Truce?"

Alice backed off a step and glared at her. Not trusting. Still on guard.

Katie remained ready, too, not sure whether the pause might be to inhale some fresh air and build up steam. Wary, like animals they watched each other. Standing still as statues, hate and fury glowed in the unflinching eyes of each girl. Then, a barely perceptible nod from Alice. As if on cue, the two girls turned away from each other with no further communication.

Katie collected her books and as many of the papers as she could find and painfully stumbled homeward. Alice, with damaged body and wounded pride, went her own way. Both knew nothing more would pass between them.

Elementary school days continued on. The fight between Alice and Katie was not mentioned by either. Alice steered clear of Katie and Susan and they, likewise, stayed away from her. Eventually, though the incident was not forgotten, it ceased to be important. But an unshakable bond had been formed between Susan and Katie.

Through the remaining school years the two of them were like sisters. Perhaps closer than sisters: they had not been born into each other's family, rather, had chosen each other.

* * *

By high school Susan was the more out-going of the two. Katie enjoyed reading and studies more than a social life. Susan had a group of friends that hung around together. One of their favorite places to go for fun was roller-skating on Friday or

Saturday nights.

"Why don't you come along with us?" Susan urged Katie. "There are a lot of the kids you already know. We always have a great time. If you try it and really don't like it, then you don't have to come with us again. But, I think you'll have fun."

At her urging Katie finally agreed. By autumn the crowd had welcomed her. She enjoyed being a 'regular' and felt happy to belong.

As the weekend approached the group went to the rink and skated for hours. Few were old enough to drive. None of them had a car. Parents would take turns driving them to and from the rink. At first, Katie's parents, never offering to play chauffeur, would provide money for her to rent skates and buy some snacks. Finding that a nuisance, they started giving her an allowance, 'to take care of things like that', so they needn't be bothered.

Most of the kids owned their skates and it was traditional for the girls to wear very short skating skirts with coordinating 'bloomers' and blouse. The mother of one of Katie's friends was an excellent seamstress and offered to make Katie a skating outfit for her birthday. Since fittings were necessary Katie could see it as it progressed. She thought it was beautiful and was thrilled, thinking how nice it would look when she wore it to the rink. Her birthday was only a week away.

One evening after dinner, before her parents went into the living room to discuss their day's activities, Katie managed to take her mother aside.

"Mother," Katie pleaded, "I really would love to have my own rink skates. I know they're expensive, but I get very good grades, and do my chores. And my birthday is almost here. Don't you think that would make a terrific birthday present?"

"I'm sure it would, dear," her mother responded absentmindedly.

"Well, then, will you get them for me?"

"We'll see, Katie, we'll see."

That certainly was better than a flat 'no'. Katie held out hope that there would be a box, wrapped or not, containing soft, white leather skates with rubber toe-stops.

Her birthday morning she found a note on the kitchen counter. Just a note. Not even a card: 'Your father and I have a meeting tonight after work so don't wait up for us.'

No mention of birthday, nor of skates. *Maybe they're playing a trick on me. They'll be home at the usual time with the surprise and it'll be wonderful.*

But they weren't. And the next day there still was no comment about either. Months went by before Katie was able to get over her deep disappointment. Yet, she continued to go skating with the crowd. As before, she rented skates.

CHAPTER SIX

Time went on its merry way. Katie began to mature into an attractive young woman. Not a knock-out, but good features, a head full of shiny brown curls and the slender body of an athlete.

Most of her waking hours continued to revolve around school. Her straight-A report cards had become so commonplace that, although she didn't slack off, she no longer felt the intense pride in her grades that she once had.

She became a cheerleader for the boys Varsity football team. She played on girls Junior Varsity, then Varsity, volleyball and softball teams, twice being chosen MVP in softball. She sang in the chorus.

Between Katie's practices, games and homework, and her parent's jobs and travel plans they were more like distant roommates than anything else. There was virtually no communication between them. It seemed that the only true conversation was about absolute necessities such as holidays. No one made waves. Life followed the same path. As a family they drifted even further apart.

Katie graduated Valedictorian of her class and accepted a scholarship to The University of Maryland. Her parents were spending time in London and missed the event.

* * *

She'd had several friends through the years but Susan was the only constant in Katie's life. They remained friends year in and year out. Susan now worked as a receptionist in a Silver Spring law firm. Still haunted by the ill-fitting, out of style, hand-me-down clothes she'd worn in elementary school she splurged her first paychecks on new things to wear. Once she had a decent wardrobe, she began a night course at a secretarial school.

Although their lives had taken drastically different directions and their schedules conflicted greatly, Katie and Susan managed to keep in touch. Neither was what you would call a social butterfly.

Katie had never been on a date. The few boys who had either worked up the courage to ask her out, or had asked her out on a dare, had been turned down, to their mixed emotions of relief and insult. Although Katie was pleasant and cordial to nearly everyone, she kept her distance from boys. Most of them believed she was stuck-up. She seemed reserved and was considered rather aloof.

She really wasn't that way at all. Having been pushed aside by her parents throughout her short life, Katie had no idea of how to approach a one-on-one relationship. Group events were just fine, thank you. The only area she was insecure: matters of the heart. Not only did she have no idea of what to expect, she was afraid of getting hurt.

While in the girl's bathroom at school she'd often seen someone crying because her boyfriend had dumped her. There was safety in numbers and school events satisfied her social needs.

* * *

Susan, on the other hand, had dated quite a lot. Unfortunately, the guys she went out with couldn't talk. Not that they were mutes. They did know the English language. They just couldn't carry on a conversation. A movie, a burger, a kiss goodnight and maybe trying to cop a feel seemed to be the universal idea of a swell time.

Susan wanted more than that. To talk. To listen. She sort of liked the kiss good night. Even the feel had possibilities. But the trade-off of general boredom hardly seemed worth it. She would much rather have spent a couple of hours in intelligent, or at a minimum, amusing conversation.

A choice would be to go into D.C. on Saturday or Sunday and visit the Smithsonian. Or the Corcoran Art Gallery. Or the Capitol Building. There were dozens of neat places to go in Washington, many of them free. After all it was the capitol of the country and pretty much of the world. Plenty was going on there all the time. But no such luck. *What's the matter with me? These guys that ask me out do not have a brain between them*

CHAPTER SEVEN

Katie's schedule was busy, busy, busy. In spite of herself, in the beginning she was overwhelmed by the University of Maryland. It seemed huge. Not at all like high school. Massive red brick Colonial-style buildings scattered across acres and acres of lush green lawn. And so many students. Her independent nature assured her she'd take this in stride once she settled in to the size and pace. This held promise of adventure.

The adventure it became proved to be an exciting one. This building at seven-forty-five a.m. for English Lit. Next class, not for three hours at another building. Three classes crammed into the next day before 1:00. So much to learn. So much to do. Something going on all the time. Katie decided that next semester she'd move onto campus and regretted not living there already. Little time as possible was spent at home. Nothing was there for her besides occasional meals and laundry facilities. Hard to decide which might be the more important of the two.

Several weeks passed as she adjusted to college. Such a variety of people. From those who seemed so sophisticated and worldly with perfect makeup, clothes from Saks, and no hair out of place, to the laid-back hippie-style group who wore ragged jeans and tee shirts and straggly hair. Young, old, many nationalities, all sorts in between. Some acted careless, but most were there to get an education.

Katie had trouble controlling her eagerness to be everywhere, see and do everything. These new emotions surfaced and she had no idea why, or what, if anything, she should do about it. Katie knew she could hold her own academically, but she'd be no match to those who were used to playing the male-female game of dating. She'd never spent much time thinking about it. This was beginning to change.

She managed to be intelligent, feminine, and athletic simultaneously. None infringing on the other. It was a pleasant combination that she happily took for granted. So much so that she wasn't aware those were the very qualities that attracted others to her. Many students seemed to enjoy being around her and wanted to make friends with her. She had never experienced such a surge of popularity. Although surprising and yet somewhat confusing, she enjoyed it. She didn't have a conniving bone in her body and was much too open and innocent for her own good.

Metamorphosis was under way. Slowly, but surely, Katie began to emerge from her protective shell. Time had come to test her wings. She didn't rush headlong into the social swirl but she accepted a date here and there. Being very selective about who she went out with, it was seldom the same guy twice.

She got the nickname 'Kid' because of her age and inexperience. Her initial reaction, to that, was that her feelings were hurt. Then she realized no one had malicious intent. It was all in fun. They liked her. She relaxed and felt good about it.

Unlike high school, extra curricular activities fell by the wayside. No clubs. No cheerleading. No chorus. Studying to keep her grades up, and indulging in this new social whirl, took all her time. So the grades remained in first place, dating in second, and the other activities a weak third. Her priorities had decidedly changed over the months at Maryland.

It was great to sit in the stands cheering for the Terrapins, win or lose. Homecoming was an *event*. There were dances, parties in the dorms. She went to them all. Usually with a different date. In spite of her new-found free spirit she didn't feel at all ready for anything even slightly serious. Until she was near the end of her freshman year. Until she met Kenny Hagen.

Kenny just sort of fell out of the sky. A knight in shining armor ready to rescue a damsel in distress.

CHAPTER EIGHT

As Katie drove her little yellow Pinto along the 495 Beltway to the University she heard a tapping noise coming from under the hood of the car. Although distracting, it didn't seem to be affecting anything. Now halfway there, she decided not to worry about it and to continue on to school.

With only a few miles to go she noticed a light in the dash click on and glow red. Dammit. The heat indicator. *What's the matter? This car is almost new. Nothing should be wrong!*

If there was any area Katie was totally weak in it most certainly was mechanics. Not one thing mechanical interested her. Cars, least of all. You filled it with gas. Periodically had an oil change. Routine maintenance. This done, barring wrecking it, a car should last forever. It took you from point A to point B. Then back again. Boring.

What did that stupid red light mean? Pull over to the side, that's what. Obviously, the radiator. Overheating. Clicking on the turn signal she edged her way into the right lane, then onto the shoulder. Katie sat there steaming, right along with the engine. The next exit might not have a gas station or car repair place that would be close enough to be of help.

At least it was daytime. She got out of the car, thinking she'd raise the hood. Steam poured out the edges. Nope. Not a chance she'd touch that.

Katie stood for a moment contemplating what direction to head. She'd have to walk. Which way to the nearest exit? Who would have a pay phone? As she toyed with her decision, a bright blue tow truck materialized on the shoulder. It stopped behind her little yellow car. A young man stepped out, a cigarette dangled from his lips.

"Need some help?" he asked.

"Well, I guess so," Katie answered. "This silly thing is being temperamental."

"Just like a woman," he said, and laughed.

"Or a man," Katie countered.

Their eyes met for a moment and Katie felt flustered. Feeling the warmth of a blush begin, she looked away quickly. "Can you, uh, figure out what's wrong with it?" she asked, pointing to her vehicle.

He had not missed her awkwardness and found it amusing. "Prob'ly. I can figure out almost anything that's got to do with cars. Let's get the hood up."

Katie stood back and watched as pulled on gloves and raised the hood. More steam billowed out.

"We'll let it set a bit," he said. "It's purty hot. Did ya hear anything while ya was drivin' along?"

The poor English grated on her nerves. Still, there was *something* about him.

"Well, there was this noise," she said. "Uh, sort of tapping or something, just for a couple of minutes. Then the little red light on the dash came on."

She studied him, trying to be casual about it. He looked quite ordinary in every way. Conservatively cut brown hair. A rather squarish face with a hint of whiskers. Straight non-descript nose. Brown eyes that held a twinkle and suggested a sense of humor might be present. Average height. Maybe five-ten or eleven. A guess put him at about one-ninety with some muscle, but not a body builder for sure. A nice combination.

He smoked. She didn't care for that, but she could deal with it. *Listen to me, I'm assessing him as if he's a house I'm considering buying.* What in the world was it about him and why should she care? He certainly was no Paul Newman. But, then, Newman smoked.

"Yeah, okay. Prob'ly the fan belt. I'll take a look when it's done spittin' steam out and cools down some."

With nothing more to be said they stood on the shoulder till the car cooled enough inside so he could reach in and touch things without getting blistered. He carefully slid his hand behind the radiator and after a little tug extracted a length of stringy black rubber. He held it up, making it wiggle like a snake, and smiled.

"One fan belt. I'm surprised it didn't fall outta the bottom. That's what ya heard. It was flappin' around inside."

"Can you fix it?" asked Katie.

"I can't fix the fan belt but I can put a new one on for ya." he said.

"Will you need to tow it?"

"Well, I could. Or we can just go down the road and get a new belt and come back here and I'll put it on. Don't need a rack. I've got the tools. Ain't no big deal."

"All right, that sounds fine." Then as an afterthought, "How much will it cost?"

"Well, the belt is only a coupla bucks but I'll have to charge ya ten for a road call. Still, that's better than if I hadda tow ya.

That'd be twenny-five just for the tow."

Katie's senses were acting up. "Shall I ride along with you?" She wondered if she sounded as eager as she felt.

He looked at her and displayed a lop-sided grin, his brown eyes twinkling. "Didn't ya momma ever tell ya not to get into a car with a strange man?"

Blushing again and feeling confused, Katie said, "That's a truck not a car. And are you a strange man?" What in god's name was she saying? The words just spilled out unbidden. She wanted to kick herself. This was not the Katie she was used to being.

"Nah, I'm not strange," he said. "Hop in."

It was a high step up. He helped her in although she could have managed on her own. Her mini skirt hiked up some. She tugged it down.

He grinned again. "Nice legs," he said.

He walked around the cab and swung up into the driver's seat. Lighting another cigarette, he gunned the engine and they were on their way. In more than one direction.

* * *

By the time the new belt had been installed Katie had learned that his name was Kenny Hagen. He was born in Washington DC and was twenty-five years old. His father had been a mailman as long as Kenny could remember, his mother a waitress at one of the nicer downtown restaurants.

School held little interest for him. He'd quit in the eleventh grade, got a job pumping gas, intending it to be temporary. However, the mechanic working there took a liking to him, and taught him a wealth about cars and car repair. Now, if someone told him the symptoms, he could figure it out and repair almost any American made car. And, if parts were available, many of the foreign ones as well.

He knew cars. He loved cars. He was a full-fledged mechanic and hoped to have his own shop some day. Strictly repairs. No gas or other frills. He'd had a girlfriend, Lizzie, a while back, but she'd dumped him and then seemed to disappear off the face of the earth. So he was in no hurry for another. His favorite music was country. He and his best friend, Elwood, shared an apartment.

What was her attraction to him? They had little, if anything, in common. They didn't even like the same kind of music. Still...

CHAPTER NINE

Katie called Susan. Susan had more moxie when it came to men. The young women were within a few months of being the same age but Susan understood relationships. She'd dated for years, discarding many men along the way as being 'unacceptable'. Plus, Susan was no longer a virgin. She knew what this sex thing was all about. She'd met a lawyer, named Joe, and they'd dated off and on for months. Within a year or so they became lovers and were seriously considering living together. After all, this was 1978 and that sort of lifestyle was commonplace. He wanted to marry Susan but she wasn't ready yet for that complete a commitment.

"Go figure. It's usually the guy that gets cold feet," he complained to anyone who would listen. But he accepted it and was more than willing to wait till she felt the time was right. He adored her.

"Susan," asked Katie, "are you going to be around tonight?"

Susan detected urgency in her friend's voice. "I have school," she said, "but I'll be home about nine-fifteen or so. Want to come by then, or is that too late?"

"No, that'll be good. I just need to talk to you."

"What's up?" Susan asked. "You're not in trouble or anything are you?"

"In trouble? Me? No. Just confused. I need my big sister."

Susan chuckled at the 'big sister'. She asked, "What is it, a man?"

"Why would you ask that?"

"Well, if it was anything else you wouldn't need help to figure out what's going on in your head. You'd solve it on your own. You're the cool one. I'm the one who comes to you with *my* problems. You usually think it through and have all the right answers. Anyhow, it is a man, isn't it?"

"Yes," said Katie. "It is."

"Good for you. It's about time. You need more experience with men. See you tonight."

They hung up and Katie felt better. Then she felt worse. Then she didn't know how she felt. She wasn't even sure what the problem was or how she could describe it to Susan. Whatever, Susan would understand. She knew about men.

* * *

"So," said Susan. "What's going on? You've met a guy?"

"Yes."

"Tell me all about it. Where did you meet him? What's he like?"

"Well, a while back, my car acted up when I was on the way to school. It overheated and steam poured out from under the hood. I had to pull off the beltway onto the shoulder. I had no idea what to do."

"How did this guy get into the picture? Does he have a name?"

"A tow truck pulled onto the shoulder behind me. The driver saw I had a problem and stopped to help. His name's Kenny."

"Okay. He helped you?" What did he do?

"He knew right away what was wrong. And that it needed a new fan belt. He didn't have the part with him."

"So he couldn't fix it after all? He drove off and just left you sitting there?"

"Oh, no. Not at all. He explained that he could tow my car to the station. Or he could go there and get the part and come back to put it on. Then I'd be on my way. Towing was more expensive. So I opted for the second choice."

"Well, that makes sense. But, of course there's more."

"Yeah, he suggested I ride along to the station with him, in his truck."

"Ah, now it's getting interesting."

"There wasn't much to it. I went along, he got the part and we went back to put it on."

"So, what is it then?"

"I got terribly flustered. And felt foolish. It seemed like we were flirting. Both of us. Can you imagine me flirting?"

"Stranger things have happened."

"I learned a lot about him. Even the name of his ex-girlfriend. Her name was Lizzie. I remember that because the only other Lizzie I ever heard of was the Lizzie Borden woman. You know the rhyme: 'Lizzie Borden took an ax…' I can't imagine what I even see in him. Our backgrounds are completely different. And he has no education. Yet…there's this attraction I don't understand. Well, you know."

They talked and drank tomato juice and snacked on Ritz crackers and chunks of cheese till after midnight. In the final analysis, they decided that this thing with Kenny was only a test of boundaries on both parts. After all, she'd just met him. And since Katie wasn't proficient in the art of figuring out what motivated a man, that's what accounted for her strange emotions and nervousness. Kenny, on the other hand, being older and more experienced, had just been teasing with her. This settled, the two young women walked out into the cool night air to Katie's car.

"Still confused?" Susan asked Katie.

"A little, but I'll get over it."

"Don't try, go with the flow. Could be fun. Maybe it's love at first sight. Or first fright."

Katie laughed. Then, "Well, he emphasized 'ex' as in ex-girlfriend. So I assumed he wasn't currently involved with someone. Susan, I thought we decided it's probably nothing. Don't put thoughts in my head."

"Key word here: *probably*," said Susan. "He's got your phone number, right? So just wait and see what happens. Or…make something happen yourself."

"Oh, crap," said Katie. "More to think about. See you later."

They hugged, said their goodnights and Katie drove off.

* * *

A week went by. Then another. Kenny didn't call. The first week she thought about him a lot. The second week, not as often. Of course she knew where he worked. It was just a gas station and she could easily stop there and fill the tank. That would take nerve she didn't have. She didn't want to be that obvious.

Monday, the beginning of the third week, he called. He

talked on and on about cars. This Chevy. That Ford. How he'd just bought Mags for his own car— with locks so they wouldn't get stolen. So far as she was concerned he may as well have been talking in tongues. But she didn't care that he was talking cars, cars, cars, she was just happy that he'd finally called. They'd been off the phone for an hour before she realized he hadn't even suggested a date.

The phone rang again. Eagerly she lifted the receiver. It was Susan. "Hey, any news?"

Katie related what the conversation with Kenny had been like.

"Well, if you ask me," said Susan, "maybe he's not worth the effort. You two don't really seem to have interests that work together anyway. But," she giggled, "you know the old saying: opposites attract."

"Why do you keep adding 'but' to so many things?" asked Katie.

"Well, you always need to have a little space. Not much is absolute. Anything is possible."

Kenny called again Tuesday. Then Wednesday. The subject matter, cars, never changed much. Simply hearing his voice was enough for Katie. For the time being.

CHAPTER TEN

Kenny called regularly for several weeks. Then one night he called with a surprise. "Hey, Katie, wanna go out with me Saturday night?"

"Oh. Well, where? What do you have in mind?"

"I've got a great idea."

"You're not going to tell me?"

"Nah, it's special. Y'all love it."

"Well...I don't know."

"Sure ya will. How 'bout it?"

Wanting to see him again, Katie agreed.

Saturday, at five o'clock, Katie stood peeking out her window anxiously waiting for Kenny to get there. It had been two months since she first met him. She hadn't seen him even once. Watching him drive up in his blue Ford Mustang she wanted to race to answer the bell. But, when his horn announced his arrival, she used control and walked out casually instead. *Silly me, why did I think he might come up to the door?*

Katie slid onto the seat next to him. His grin set his eyes twinkling and he said simply, "Hiya, kid, all set?"

She nodded and replied, "Sure, let's go." *This really is no good. He just jumbles my mind.*

Kenny smiled, put the car in gear and took off.

"Ready for the surprise?" he asked.

"I am. Tell me what it is."

"Can'tcha guess?"

"I've tried, but I have no idea. So you need to let me know."

"Well, we're going into D.C."

"And then?"

"Ya'll see." His smile glowed smug and happy.

The drive through D.C. was easy and pleasant. Kenny chattered about his work and about cars. By the time they reached the Armory Katie began to feel excited. Kenny parked on the street and they walked half a block to the building, holding hands the whole way. Then she saw the sign outside: **Annual Auto Show, Saturday and Sunday 12 noon – 12 midnight.**

She gasped. "This is it? The surprise?"

"Yeah, ain't it amazing? A whole buildin' full of all different kind of cars. Old, new, everything ya can dream of. Yer gonna love it!"

The shiny automobiles were impressive. Even Katie had to admit that. Brand new cars glittered under the bright overhead spotlights. Older cars, that had been customized to the point of anyone's wildest dreams, sparkled. Kenny oozed excitement. He lovingly touched a '56 Chevvy that had metal-flake paint that shimmered after many coats of wax. The fake fur upholstery of another was soft and lush. Every inch of chrome on each of them was polished to a mirror finish. He fairly drooled over them. Cars. His love.

Although Katie thought they were pretty—not a word Kenny would use to describe them—she couldn't come close to experiencing the thrill he displayed. Though she found it amusing, it was beyond her imagination how someone could get so thoroughly enamored with a cold piece of metal. They did look good, but all in all, a car was simply a means of transportation.

Without serious regret, trying to place it into the category of a learning experience, she let Kenny lead her from one car to another, as he described in great detail, techniques used to modify some of the vehicles. He acted like a child at Christmas.

Don't think I'll go out with this one again.

By eleven o'clock Kenny had pretty well examined every car in the place. "Let's go get a pizza," he suggested.

Suddenly hungry, Katie agreed. They headed back toward Maryland, stopping at a pizza place called Mom's & Pop's. It wasn't a glamorous restaurant, but the lighting was dim and the booth they were seated in made it more cozy and private. Conversation should have flowed. All the elements seemed correct. Yet Katie couldn't think of a thing to say that would be of interest to them both and Kenny seemed content to give the pizza his undivided attention.

With the pizza devoured there was little reason to hang around. Kenny paid the tab and they left. Back in the car Kenny jiggled the radio dial and, finding nothing to please him, slipped an old Hank Williams cassette into the player. He sang along with the music as he drove. Every now and then he'd reach over and squeeze Katie's knee and flash that lopsided grin.

He was in a good mood. The evening had been fun—seeing all those beautiful machines, filling up on pizza, and this attractive girl sitting next to him. He glanced over at Katie. "Ya sure don't talk much, fer a girl," he said.

"What's there to say about cars that you haven't already

said?" Katie asked.

"True fact. I did go on about 'em didn't I?"

"Well, it seems there is absolutely nothing in the world that you find interesting or important but cars."

"There really ain't much that gets to me the way a fine car can. But, there is one other thing that's been takin' up some space in my mind lately."

"What's that?" asked Katie without a clue of what the answer could be.

"Not really a 'what', a 'who'."

"Oh," said Katie, only mildly disappointed that it couldn't be her and assuming that was the reason he'd talked only about cars—a neutral and safe subject. "Anybody I know?"

"Yup. It's you," he said, turning his head and grinning at her. And with that, he stopped his car right in the middle of Georgia Avenue. As angry horns blared from behind he planted a firm kiss squarely on her lips. Without a word he put the car back in gear and continued on as though nothing out of the ordinary had happened.

Katie, surprised, happy, and angry all at once, sat speechless.

"Now, don't be mad," said Kenny. "I just had to do that!"

"It's okay," Katie said softly, her mind in a whirl.

They rode the rest of the way in silence, each lost in their own unusual thoughts.

CHAPTER ELEVEN

Though no commitments of any sort had been made, Kenny, without discussion, considered Katie 'his girl'. Not questioning it or understanding why, Katie accepted it. He nicknamed her "Kates". Almost immediately, they began to see each other several times a week. In spite of many and extreme differences a closeness developed and each felt good having someone to hang out with and depend on.

* * *

As time went by Kenny promised to make an attempt to learn and be interested in the things she wanted to do and talk about. Katie knew full well that it would be a difficult, if not impossible, task to get him to understand how she felt about her education. More so, to discuss things that went on in the world, and life in general. But she was very willing to try. They needed a common ground. It would be wonderful if she could help him find something that intrigued him besides cars. She believed she could educate him. Bring him up a bit intellectually so they would have a variety of things to enjoy together. There's a huge difference between being uneducated and stupid. Kenny was not stupid.

Katie acknowledged this would be a two-way street. If he sincerely tried to understand her world, she would have to try to spark an interest in his: cars. She borrowed books from the library that provided information on car maintenance and repair. Finding the subject boring, she often fell asleep while trying to read them. But she continued to put forth the effort. Little by little she made some headway by learning a few basics: how to change a flat tire if she had to, replace windshield wiper blades, check the oil level in her car and add a can of oil if needed.

She began to comprehend the need and use of various car parts she'd barely heard the name of before. For instance: the carburetor. She read that it mixed gas with air to produce spontaneous combustion to run the engine. Without understanding how it did that, she thought she might be able to learn. Coming across the word 'differentials' did it. Way over her head. A new respect for the vocation of a car mechanic began to bloom.

Throughout the summer they spent three, four, five evenings a week together. During the day Kenny worked at the gas station. Katie accepted a full-time summer job doing research for a medical firm.

Wanting to impress Kenny, she continued to try to memorize the make and model of vehicles she saw on the road. This worked with some success until Kenny discovered she was reading the information displayed on the car. He laughed at her and told her not to worry about remembering all those names. He'd take care of that.

During the process of trying to learn from, and about, each other there were times Kenny got angry with her. He'd accuse her of trying to 'show-off her smarts' and make him feel like he was stupid. Then, while smoking one cigarette after another, he'd drive her home in silence, mumbling goodbye as Katie got out of the car. It would be two or three days, maybe longer, before he'd call again. No matter how much she wanted to talk to him, to apologize or clear up any misunderstanding, her stubborn streak prevailed. The phone sat idle.

Several times though, glancing out the front window, she'd caught a glimpse of a blue car drive slowly by. She couldn't be sure, but wondered if it might be him.

When he did call he acted as though nothing unusual had happened and ask, "Hey, Kates, do ya wanna go get a pizza?"

Each time, covering her hurt and anger, Katie would say, "Sure, why not?"

So went the emotional waves of summer. With the end of July around the corner, time for Katie to return to the University of Maryland approached rapidly. From now on, she'd live on campus. Her parent's empty house could stay that way.

CHAPTER TWELVE

Settling into the first few weeks of her junior year left little time to spend with Kenny. There were books to buy and a new routine to adjust to. She'd added another class to her already busy schedule. That meant extra studying.

"Come on, Kates," Kenny said, "We're missin' out on too much. Get this stuff in order so we can get on back to *our* routine."

Even though complaining, he did it with that smile. Katie realized how much she'd missed him, too. Since August they'd only been together a few times and here it was the beginning of October.

* * *

Wednesdays were Katie's lightest day at college. One particular Wednesday glowed with typical Indian Summer weather: temperature in the low eighties, but comfortable, with no humidity to speak of. Kenny took half the day off work. Together they packed a paper bag with a full lunch: sandwiches, chips, fruit, cookies and sodas, and headed to Rock Creek Park for a picnic. They sat across from one another at an old wooden table with a bench attached to each side.

The weathered tabletop felt rough from the initials of past friends and lovers that had been carved into the wood. Kenny pulled a pocketknife from his Levis and carefully added 'K & K' to the collection. He surrounded that with a crudely etched heart. Katie watched as he performed his art. When it was complete, she simply said, "Kenny, thank you for that. It's so sweet."

He folded the blade back into position and tucked the knife in his pocket smiling all the while.

With lunch finished and trash in the nearby container, Kenny extinguished his cigarette. Hand in hand they wandered through the woods on the well-traveled soft, earth pathway. The brilliant fall colors Mother Nature had selected to trim the trees brought comfort. Things seemed to be the way they should be. A good omen.

* * *

The creek rushed around and over rocks, splashing and bubbling along only a few feet from the path. In many areas you could get from one side of the creek to the other by navigating carefully, using rocks as stepping-stones. The water was shallow in most places, so if you lost your footing and slipped in, small chance you'd get very wet or hurt.

The narrow walkway opened up to a wider and particularly pretty spot displaying, among other things, a huge rock. Really more of a boulder. Climbing up onto it they sat and listened to the water as it gently slapped against the bank. What a day. Everything was perfect. Peaceful. And, save for the gurgling creek, or an occasional bird chirping, quiet.

Kenny put an arm around her and drew her to him. He kissed her neck softly and let his fingers get lost in her curly mane. His hand drifted down her back, then under her t-shirt and upward, deftly unhooking her bra. Katie went rigid.

"Please don't do that," she said. "I've asked you a dozen times not to."

"Ya know I love ya, Kates," said Kenny. "And I want ya."

"And you know I can't do that," Katie said. "I just can't. I don't know how and I'm scared."

"Ya said ya love me," Kenny firmly reminded her. "Dammit,

48

prove it!"

"That's not fair!" said Katie. "I *do* love you, and you know it. But this really frightens me."

"You're so damn ol'fashioned," Kenny exploded. "No one waits till they're married now days. It's no big deal! Who's gonna' know anyway? Ya think I'd hurt ya?"

Katie's eyes misted. She felt very young. Much younger than her years. *I guess he's right, I'm nearly twenty-two years old and haven't the first realistic idea about sex. Maybe I should learn.*

"Okay," she whispered, "but not now. Not here. Give me a little more time."

CHAPTER THIRTEEN

Katie couldn't work up her nerve to call Susan to ask again for advice. She felt childish and foolish and already knew how Susan felt about such things. But she needed to talk to someone. Sex was a huge step so far as she was concerned. Something you shouldn't rush into without serious thought. Other than some clinical 'book learning', she'd had no true education regarding sex. Even Susan hadn't gone into detail. Katie always discouraged such conversations. Almost as though she were afraid to even talk about it. As though she felt her innocence was in jeopardy.

Getting information from her parents was out of the question. If she asked them to explain anything personal like that, they'd be shocked. They'd never spoken the word 'sex' aloud in front of her. She certainly couldn't approach them about such a subject. Especially now. They continued along, each in their own little world, virtually unaware of Katie's existence, especially since she'd been in college. Even more so since she'd been living on campus. They did provide a generous financial stipend that Katie felt was borne by their guilt. Beyond that she considered them useless.

Sex would not be another topic of conversation with Kenny any time soon. They'd been through this many times before – the subject came up often – she thought he simply didn't understand. At first he'd been patient, but now he'd no longer even try to see her point of view. He'd get cool toward her, and angry, telling her to grow up and face life's realities. She had considered breaking up with him. But that was not at all what she wanted to do.

She felt very un-grownup. It was as though her time as a child had been spent as an adult, and now, as an adult, she behaved childishly. Was this sex-thing so important? She'd experienced urges, too, but always dismissed the feelings and easily kept them under control. What was the big hurry? The issue seemed to be taken completely out of proportion.

Even if she had a confidant to guide or advise her, the final decision would be her own. No one else could make the choice for her. But she had to do something. If she chose to go along with Kenny's ideas she'd need some information. And some protection. She picked up the phone and called Dr. Lorenzo's office. By pleading a sore throat, she got an appointment for the next day.

At three-fifteen Katie sat nervously on a gray vinyl-covered chair in the examination room waiting for Dr. Lorenzo to come in. The room had an antiseptic scent that was neither pleasant nor unpleasant. Simply an odor all medical offices seemed to have. She surveyed the array of supplies and equipment neatly arranged on the white metal cart near the examining table: a glass jar full of tongue depressors; another with extra long cotton swabs; shiny metal utensils for use undetermined by Katie; bottles of assorted liquids, uniformly labeled and lined up like miniature brown, glass soldiers. Nothing looked terribly ominous. And no indication of the true purpose of her visit.

Presently the door opened and in strode Dr. Lorenzo, a stethoscope hanging around his neck. Katie felt, by the way he walked, the way he stood with his shoulders squared and posture erect, that he was sure he had chosen the correct profession. He bore an air of confidence. The warmth of his frequent smile was sincere and, as always, further assured Katie, that he liked who he was and what he did. Dr. Lorenzo had delivered Katie over two decades ago and now continued to be her doctor. She trusted him.

He was a modern doctor and took pride in staying in tune with the times and the people. His one throwback to the old days was that he still wore the white, crisply starched, loose jacket that most of the younger medical professionals scorned in favor of a business shirt and tie.

"Well, Katie," he began, "let's have a look at that throat." He picked up a tiny flashlight and selected a tongue depressor from the glass jar. He flipped his head-mirror down and waited.

Katie looked down, kept her mouth closed, and sat still.

Dr. Lorenzo, perceptive, teased a little. "Come on, now, open up." He studied her expression.

Katie lifted her chin, started to open her mouth then stopped. The doctor pitched the tongue depressor into the wastebasket and placed the flashlight back on the cart. With a genuinely concerned expression he questioned softly, "Why are you really here? It isn't your throat at all, is it?"

"I..," Katie stammered, and fell silent. Dr. Lorenzo waited.

"I..," she started again. "I would like a prescription for birth control pills," she finally blurted out.

"Well, is that all?" he smiled. "I guess we're at the wrong end for an examination for that." He tried to get a grin from her. Help her to relax.

"I'll need to do a pelvic." He handed her a paper robe. "Undress, put this on, open to the front. You can lay your clothes on the chair. I'll get my things and be right back." He left the room. Feeling like a robot, Katie stripped and donned the paper robe.

Returning with the necessary equipment, he tapped lightly

on the door as a courtesy, before entering the room. Although she lay rigid as a board, he conducted the exam quickly, and pronounced Katie to be in fine condition. Peeling off the latex gloves he tossed them into the receptacle.

Just chatting, he said, "Glad it wasn't anything serious. There seems to be quite a number of cases of mono this year and one of the early signs is a sore throat."

"Is that all there is to it?" Katie asked, ignoring the remark about mono, often referred to as the kissing disease.

"Do you think there should be more?"

"Don't you need to ask any questions or anything?"

"I have your medical history. From even *before* you were born. That's all *I* need. I expect there may be more *you* need. Is there something you think I should know? Or even something I shouldn't know, that you just want to get off your chest? You can depend on me to respect your privacy. I've known you all your life. You're like a daughter."

Katie thought a moment then shook her head. "No, " she said. "There's nothing. Thanks anyway."

"Well, Katie, just remember a couple of things: I'm here if you need me, and, whatever you decide won't change who you are or what you are, unless you let it."

Katie pondered this for a second or two. Then, "Thanks again,"

"Okay, go ahead and get dressed. Call back next week and I'll let you know the results. Assuming all is well, and I have no reason to think it isn't, I'll call a prescription in to People's Drug Store for you."

CHAPTER FOURTEEN

Katie stood in front of the wood-framed mirror that hung on the wall above her dresser. She studied the reflection that stared back at her. She didn't look any different.

"What did you expect?" the face in the glass asked her. *"Did you really believe that you would be covered with little green dots or that a flashing neon sign would appear across your forehead?"*

She smiled. The other face smiled back at her.

"No," Katie told the image. "Of course not. I didn't really believe it would show." She was being silly. No one could tell a thing by looking at her. The change was not on the outside, it was on the inside. She did feel differently. Not quite sure how, only that it wasn't the same.

If anything, she felt a little disappointed. This thing called sex seemed highly over-rated. Actually, it had been pretty nice once she'd overcome her severe nervousness and allowed herself to relax. But by then it was over. On the other hand, it wasn't all that great, either. Most certainly not the consuming thrill she'd been led to believe. There must be more to it.

Walking across the room she stood facing the full-length mirror attached to her closet door. She posed in front of it trying to analyze her looks. No movie star, but pleasant enough. Maybe she should cut her hair. It was too curly, and nearly down to the middle of her back now. She'd begun to feel like a carbon copy of every other young female around.

Katie unzipped her jeans and slid them down. She tucked a foot under the waistband, lifted them and tossed them out of the way. Watching herself in the mirror she saw long legs, shapely enough to require a second glance, she supposed. Lifting her t-shirt slightly she turned around to view the reflection of her bottom clad in light blue bikini panties with a pattern of darker blue hearts scattered about. She frowned. *Maybe a little too much there.* She pulled her t-shirt over her head, letting it fall to the floor. Her breasts, a nice size, encased in a soft lacy bra, were okay. All in all, the total picture was a satisfactory one. She looked no different today than she had a week ago. A month ago. Two months ago. Good.

I have all the proper parts. She turned away from the mirror, stooped and picked up her clothes. *Why didn't I feel wonderful having sex?*

Yet, strangely enough, considering her numerous protestations to Kenny, she felt neither guilt nor remorse. Nor happiness. She thought it likely they'd try it again. No big hurry. She really wasn't very eager.

They did try it again. And again, and again. It was like the potato chip commercial "betcha can't have just one". They developed a smoothness until they moved in unison. Kenny wasn't inventive, nor was he a good teacher, but he did have natural instincts and each time Katie understood more about it. Then one day, with surprising awareness, she realized her earlier fears and inhibitions had disappeared.

This sex thing awakened sensations in her she didn't know were there. She was almost angry with Kenny for pulling these powerful feelings out of her. In the same thought, she loved him for it. Yet always felt hungry for improvement. How did one tap into the high-voltage sexual chemistry?

Kenny acted so surprised by the change in her behavior that it amused her. She'd heard that sex and love are not synonymous and that it can be very easy to confuse the two emotions. Not believing that was true, she felt happy. And terrified. She'd fallen into the strange new land called love.

Time flew. Months later, when Kenny suggested they get married, her fascination danced between excitement and thrill.

CHAPTER FIFTEEN

With only a year remaining until she finished college, they felt they could manage on Kenny's salary. She'd get a job after her senior year. They decided on a June ceremony. The wedding would be a small one inviting only their parents and a very few close friends. Kenny would take a week off work and they'd have a brief honeymoon.

Excited, Katie announced their plans to her parents. They took it calmly, almost with disinterest. Their attitude was: do what you're going to do, girl. Just do it quickly without disturbing our routine so all of us can continue our lives without missing a beat. It didn't surprise Katie, but left her disappointed. She'd foolishly harbored the notion this would be the one thing they'd show an interest in.

Susan was happy for her, although with some reservations. "Katie, I'm all for this if it's truly what you *want*. Just think it through. You know you haven't had much experience with relationships."

"Come on, Susan, what are you talking about? Kenny is thoughtful. He watches out for me. Now and then he'll just turn up someplace I happen to be. Isn't that protecting me? Besides I've dated dozens of guys in the past couple of years. It's not like this is the first guy I ever went out with."

"Yeah, well, that doesn't mean you had any relationships. You just had dates. Some fun with a guy. How many of them did you go out with more than once?"

"Maybe a few. I did go out with Steven a couple of times," said Katie. "I can't think of anyone else right now, though."

"Okay, just be sure this is what you want. And, just a

thought: are you sure Kenny's watching out *for* you? Or just *watching* you?"

In the back of her mind Susan worried that Katie might be getting married to escape her unsatisfactory family situation. On the other hand, she knew Katie's home life had always been like that. Once she'd started college she spent very little time at her parent's house and most of the time they weren't there anyway. She didn't really need to escape.

Still, Katie's behavior perplexed Susan. She felt Katie had allowed Kenny to assume total control of her life. Between Katie and Susie, Katie had always been the strong one. The confident one. The capable one. What had happened to change her like this? Susan felt uneasy with these thoughts and hoped, that when things settled down, Katie would bounce back to her old self.

"I know you believe what you're saying," said Katie, "but you'll see. I'm doing the right thing. I love Kenny and he loves me. We want to get married and what better time than now? A June wedding. It's perfect." She waved off any serious thought to Susan's advice.

Susan reluctantly stated that she, herself, might be getting soft on the issue of marriage. She admitted, "Joe and I have been looking at engagement rings. Looks like we'll be strolling down the aisle, someday soon, too." Joe and Susan had been together for more than two years now, but they hadn't rushed into marriage.

In the middle of June, at the Courthouse in Silver Spring, before the Justice of Peace, Katie Millford became Mrs. Kenneth Hagen. Within a few hours, after subdued good wishes, a beaming Katie and Kenny, headed east on Route 50 toward

Ocean City, Maryland for their honeymoon.

They unpacked and got ready to spend some time on the beach. Katie slipped on a terry-cloth cover-up concealing her new, blue-and-white striped bikini. They headed out to the beach. Once towels were spread on the sand, radio and sodas in place, Katie shrugged the cover-up off and let it slide down to her feet, and stepped out of it. She began to apply protective lotion. The bikini fit well, covering enough and not terribly skimpy. For some reason, seeing her in it angered Kenny.

He grabbed hold of her wrist, applying pressure, and said in a low voice, "Listen to this and listen well. Ya ain't gonna wear that rag ever again. Ya ain't out here to show off yer body. Yer *my* woman and no one else needs to see yer goodies."

His grip hurt her wrist. She jerked her hand away. His false accusation shocked her. It sounded so ridiculous that she had no immediate response. There'd been no such intention. The suit was similar to hundreds of others on the beach at that very moment. She glanced up at his face and knew he was serious.

Forcing herself to remain calm she took his hand. "Come on, Kenny let's have some fun. Do you want to test the ocean first, or should we build a sand castle?"

Katie hoped Kenny's outburst was a result of the stress they'd been under while making wedding plans and that nothing like this would ever happen again. She'd try to make light of it. They had selected the sun and sand of the ocean for their honeymoon and here they were.

Kenny rejected her offer of rubbing sun block on his back and shoulders. As a result he got sunburned and ended up cross and irritable the balance of the trip. Katie would not let that drag her into an ugly mood, too. One of them had to remain sane.

That evening, at a restaurant for dinner, Katie ordered seafood. Kenny, ordering steak, said, "Ya know, the fish is okay for you tonight, but ya better remember that I'm a beef and potatoes man. Don't even think about putting anything else on the table at home."

She refused to be goaded into an argument.

And so it went. Inside her head, thoughts swirled like soup being stirred in a pot. How had the man she married only a few days ago been transformed into this?

For a week that should have been one of the happiest, most memorable of their lives, it turned out to be a hideous, angry one instead. Clinging to her optimism, Katie reasoned that they both had tremendous adjustments to make and that, in time, things would work out.

Nevertheless, when the week ended and it was time to pack and go home, Katie was more than ready to leave.

Their honeymoon fell just short of complete disaster.

CHAPTER SIXTEEN

Home was to be in Silver Spring. After looking at apartments in various locations, and homes to buy, all way beyond their budget, they rented an older house. Though barely more than a cottage, it had three small bedrooms, a full basement, a nice fenced-in yard and a garage. It was suitable for their needs. And the price was right.

The owner, an elderly widower, offered a reduced rental for a period of a year in exchange for painting and minor repairs that Kenny and Katie agreed to take care of. After a discussion about an option to buy, the rental contract had been written so they must decide within three months whether they wanted to take advantage of it. They decided the option would be a good idea. They accepted the offer.

Efforts to get Kenny involved in making suggestions as to decorating their little house went in vain. He told her, "A woman's place is in the home. Fix it how ya' like it. It'll be okay. Ya'll be spending a lot more time here than I will."

Displaying his crooked, captivating smile, he lit a Marlboro and clicked the TV on to baseball. The only upholstered chair in the house had been left there by the owner. Kenny plopped into it and immediately became immersed in the Orioles game. Without as much as a glance at her asked, "How soon's dinner?"

* * *

Given the decorating go-ahead, and with weeks before college began again, Katie set out with enthusiasm to produce an attractive, comfortable place for them to share. Watching pennies would be important, for there were many true necessities. It was obvious the walls hadn't been painted in a long time. She had no doubt she could wield both a paintbrush and roller.

They'd been given a starting point: Kenny's Aunt Ruthie had offered them several odds and ends of furniture when she'd moved from her own house to a small apartment. Kenny had nothing of his own besides his bedroom furniture. Before their marriage he'd shared an apartment with his best buddy, Elwood Westbridge. The rest of the furniture there belonged to Elwood.

Aunt Ruthie's contributed sofa was a quality piece of furniture and was in very good condition. However, it seemed more appropriate for the tropics than Maryland. It was upholstered in a light green fabric patterned with huge, deep pink flowers surrounded by large, dark green leaves and made quite a statement. Katie decided that if she worked with the colors carefully a very pleasant room could develop, even though she wouldn't have chosen that particular design herself.

She closed the door to the living room and taped a sign on the outside reading: "Decorating in progress. No admittance till completed." She was eager to begin. Kenny, seeming to be back to his old self, humored her and went along with her secret project.

Her first purchase was a pale pink latex paint for the walls and the same shade in enamel for the woodwork. After measuring carefully, and armed with a paint color-chip, she shopped and ordered a room-sized rug and sheer curtains, all in deep pink. *Someday there will be wall-to-wall carpet and drapes, too.*

Katie completed painting the room in two days. The next day she hung the curtains and surveyed the area thus far. The results pleased her.

Out shopping once more, she discovered a table lamp with a dark green ceramic base and crisply pleated white shade. She bought two. She looked at chairs, but knew the budget wouldn't allow that expense right now. The one the owner left behind had a muted green stripe and would have to do for the time being. She settled for several plump floor pillows covered in lush shades of green. She headed home, satisfied with her new purchases.

Without going into great detail she shared her excitement with Susan. Her friend was so happy that things between Katie and Kenny had improved and looked forward to seeing the completed room.

Friday morning the rug was delivered and laid. By afternoon the room was finished. Katie felt proud and paced the floor the final few minutes till Kenny came home. For the past week she'd worked feverishly, keeping the door to the living room closed when Kenny was home so it would be a surprise to him when he saw how the entire project turned out. He'd thought she was being silly but to humor her went along with her plan, nonetheless. In the evenings he watched TV on the small set in the kitchen. The living room would surely be done soon.

Looking out the window she saw his car pull up. Not knowing the unveiling would be today, he showed little anticipation. Once he was inside Katie took his jacket and tossed it over the closet doorknob. Taking his hand, she pulled him toward the living room.

"You open the door," she said, excitement mounting.

"Okay," he said, flashing the old familiar lop-sided grin. Then, "Jee-*sus*! A *pink* living room!" he exploded. "Goddammit, Katie, no *man* wants a *pink* living room. Is *this* what ya been up to the whole week? A freakin' *pink* living room?"

Crushed, tears welled up in her eyes, close to spilling out. Not for a single minute had she thought this might happen. He'd seen the colors of the sofa and did not object to them. With no interest in making suggestions, he'd given her free reign to run the show. A lone tear escaped and crawled down her cheek. "Oh, Kenny, look at it. It's lovely. Give it a chance. You'll get used to it." Through misty eyes, and with a weak smile she added, "It's for us."

Kenny stood staring at the room his gaze wandering from one place to another. "I don't believe it," he muttered. "A goddam pink living room." Turning on his heel he strode toward the best room in the house, in his opinion, the kitchen.

* * *

Originally, the kitchen had been small, but adequate, opening into a seldom-used formal dining room. Several years ago the owner had been innovative and had the adjoining wall knocked down. The two rooms, remodeled into one very large, updated kitchen, offered plenty of cabinets, a nice eating space, and room for what he had called the 'conversation area'.

Kenny switched on the little portable television that sat on a serving cart in the far corner. Slumping into a chair at the table, his back to the stove where Katie stood putting finishing touches on the evening meal he asked, "What's dinner?"

"Sloppy Joes, French fries and salad," answered Katie.

"I don't want no salad," said Kenny. "The rest is okay."

Katie set the serving dishes on the table. They filled their plates and ate in silence. The only voices came from the television. The rest of the evening he chain-smoked. Katie felt that was just to irritate her and maybe get even with her over the disaster Kenny believed she'd turned the living room into. She kept her thoughts to herself not wanting to say something that might trigger an argument.

* * *

A couple of weeks dragged by before Kenny recovered from his shock and fury of the pink living room. Katie went through several stages of anger herself and only sheer determination kept her from picking a fight with Kenny. Instead, with effort, she tried to maintain a cheerful attitude and go about business as usual. She didn't *feel* cheerful but she reasoned that if she acted as though she did, sooner or later, Kenny would come around.

And, of course, he did. He still wasn't happy about the pink living room, but at least he quit complaining. The day finally came that he joked about it, often crudely and sometimes with a hint of hatefulness, but nevertheless he had become accustomed to it.

As summer came to a close their life with each other smoothed out. Living together was quite different than being lovers. At last they began to adjust to one another's ways. They were learning to be happy.

CHAPTER SEVENTEEN

Katie returned to college. Her senior year. Kenny worked with his obsession: cars. They lived on a tight budget without minding too much. Evenings were usually spent with Kenny in front of the television and Katie studying. Not exciting, but comfortable.

They both looked forward to weekends when they would share quiet time together. Sometimes they'd spend a lazy Saturday morning in bed and then have a late big breakfast. If the weather was right, the afternoon might be spent walking through Sligo Creek Park then grab something for dinner from McDonald's.

Often in the late afternoon, Elwood, Kenny's best friend, and a bunch of other buddies would come to the house. They'd hang out and play low stakes poker at the kitchen table. To Kenny's credit he always included Katie. He'd taught her the games and she was as good as any of the guys. None of them objected to her being in the game. She didn't play 'like a girl'. Besides, she brought beers to the table and removed empties; carried in a tray of snacks, and dumped out the ashtrays. What more could the guys ask for? They had a grand time and the game frequently went on till two or three in the morning and ended up with Elwood staying over.

More often Elwood would drop by the house on a Wednesday or Thursday, just for company. He'd breeze in smiling and carrying a six-pack of Bud. He had become family. Now and then they'd go out to dinner or a movie. Their social life didn't include much more, but it suited them all.

Katie and Susan made a point to get together for lunch once or twice a week. Neither commented on it but both noticed a blue car drive slowly by the restaurant they'd chosen. They each wondered if it might be Kenny checking up on them, but dismissed it as a foolish thought.

Even though she didn't mention anything to Katie, it perplexed Susan that Kenny had changed so much and Katie allowed herself to ignore it.

CHAPTER EIGHTEEN

With Katie's return to the University of Maryland she was swamped with mixed feelings. Getting a degree held the utmost importance. Her major being education, the plan of becoming a teacher never faltered. With a minor in business, that's where she expected to end up at some point in time since teachers weren't near the top of the pay scale. Especially beginners.

She remembered her own elementary school teachers well. Fondness filled her as she realized how a good teacher could make all the difference in the world. The positive influence they offered young minds and hearts often directed some students for life. It excited her to think about being in a position to guide youngsters, exposing them to knowledge and ideas as only a devout educator could.

The tumultuous summer left Katie somewhat drained although things had settled down considerably in the past month. Even those flare-ups from Kenny had decreased. Still, she felt they always lay dormant, not too deep below the surface, and that it would take little for him to explode again. But he gave no signals. That was one of the toughest parts. She didn't have a clue as to what might set him off.

* * *

Her final months at Maryland were smooth. At home, Kenny, although he'd been pounding a few more beers than usual, behaved in an acceptable way. Katie graduated Cum Laude and within a week accepted a teaching position at an elementary school a few miles from home. Kenny did not attend her graduation. Her parents, having received the announcement in the mail, sent kudos from Spain. None of it mattered to her. She was now an adult and ready to enter the real world. The burden she thought she'd been carrying, but had not been able to define, began to slip from her shoulders. Katie felt strong and independent again. Her new job began in three months. She had the entire summer to do with as she pleased.

CHAPTER NINETEEN

Life was fun again. She spent most of her time at doing what Kenny called 'wifey stuff'. Their house wasn't large and she enjoyed keeping it clean and tidy. She felt good about religiously scrubbing the bathrooms and the kitchen once a week. She made efficient use of her time and energy. It was her job. Dusting and vacuuming were easy tasks. Washing and drying dishes, not such a big deal. There were only the two of them. Although Elwood came by often he didn't use many dishes.

Laundry was another matter entirely. An old wringer-type washer, in good condition, sat by laundry tubs in the basement. There was no dryer. Well, there was a dryer: outside, in the form of clotheslines. An entire day needed to be set aside for that task. Things needed to be washed, and hung on the line by the early afternoon. If luck went her way the clothes would be dry and ready to come in before dinnertime. This wasn't a job she hated, but she knew the coming winter would present a huge challenge.

One of these days soon I'll get both an automatic washer and a dryer. Kenny will just have to deal with it. Her time could be put to better use than standing at an old-fashioned machine.

* * *

More and more often Elwood and some other of Kenny's buddies would come over on the weekend for guy talk. They'd sit around involved in friendly arguments about sports and cars, and often ended up downing a case or two of beer. They'd get rowdy while watching a football game on TV. All of them especially liked to hang out at Katie and Kenny's house because the service was good: Katie always had plenty of snacks set out and she'd take their empty beer cans away. They'd have to do nothing.

Kenny was the only one with a wife and it got to the point he enjoyed bragging about his control over her. It had started some time ago and intensified when they'd first moved into the house and Katie had been so anxious to keep it spotless. Kenny would put a cigarette out in an ashtray and swear Katie would have the butt dampened under the faucet, put into in the trash, the ashtray wiped out and returned to the end table before he even knew it was gone. He exaggerated about that, but it seemed to make him feel powerful.

Kenny teased her and called her puppy-dog because she'd do whatever he commanded of her. She might be at her desk and he'd call, "Kates, come here a minute." And she'd go to him.

He'd put a cigarette between his lips, hand her his Zippo lighter and say, "How about lighting this for me?" She'd do it. He'd laugh and say, "That's a good puppy-dog."

All sorts of things like that. In the beginning she thought it was amusing but it got old very quickly. When he pulled a stunt like that in front of others it really irritated her. If *she* mentioned how it aggravated her, especially in front of the guys, he'd explode. It was easier to go along. Let it be.

With his friends being there most weekends, Katie sometimes felt chased from her own home. She'd call Susan and they'd go to a movie or museum or shopping and their day would be fun and free of arguments. The two of them might not agree on everything, but they wouldn't call each other names and get drunk and stomp and storm.

She felt Kenny seldom realized she wasn't around unless he was looking to make a joke at her expense. Still, Katie held on to her optimism about their relationship, believing a lot of the problems would be resolved with time. They hadn't been married long and both of them had a lot of work to do in making this a success. They were very different types of people.

CHAPTER TWENTY

Beginning her chosen job provided the break they needed. Katie felt some first-year-teacher uneasiness but still confident in her skills, and thrilled to have youngsters anxious to learn. Her first assignment turned out to be six-year-olds. First grade. The prior school year they'd spent in kindergarten. Now, being away from home turned out to be an adventure for them, something to look forward to. She felt they'd no longer be weepy little kids, something Katie had worried about. She wondered if the children would like her. And she thought about the parents—would some of them look upon her as a glorified babysitter? On the other hand, some parents might resent her, thinking she'd become closer to their kids than they were.

Over-thinking now, imaginary situations crept in with her wanting to be sure she'd be able to resolve a crisis immediately: *How will I handle it if there is a bully in class? How can I divert bad behavior? What if there's a medical emergency? Who will take over if I have to go to the bathroom?*

She forced herself to settle down: *I've got this. This is what I've studied and practiced. My classroom is set up and lessons prepared. I'm dressed to impress, my shoes are comfortable and I had a good breakfast. Put me in, Coach. I'm ready to play.*

Still, first-day jitters took hold as she drove to the school. Coffee in the teachers lounge provided liquid warmth, and cordial light conversation with other teachers bolstered her confidence. Feeling genuine excitement now, she headed for her classroom. Neatly printing her name on the chalkboard satisfied her. Katie sat at her desk feeling up to the task that lay ahead.

As the bell sounded, the room filled with freshly scrubbed six-year-olds, each looking as though they wore a new first-day-of-school outfit. Chattering and laughing, bumping into one another as they entered, the clumsy stage of early childhood showed and was appealing.

Weeks flew by. Katie loved the children. They loved her. She had the perfect job.

* * *

Encouraging to those who had voted for a white Christmas, snow fell before December. In an attempt to stay ahead of the swirling flakes, road crews swarmed the streets. The blades of their plows pushed tons of the white stuff into heaps at the curbs. For the first two days traffic snarled and it seemed as though you couldn't drive a block without seeing a fender bender. Comments about the weather, ranging from 'isn't it beautiful' to 'I hate that white shit', were heard everywhere. Then, the temperature rose just enough to melt some of it, turning the piles at the curbs into ugly slush. Spray from the tires pitched crumbs of black stuff into the already hideous heaps. Snow that remained on rooftops and otherwise bare branches, glittered in lovely contrast. Yards showing no footprint sparkled like jewels. With the sun so bright, the reflection hurt your eyes even though it was beautiful to look at. Still the thermometer hovered near the freezing point. Winter ruled.

Bundled up in a heavy coat, gloves and sensible boots, Katie stopped at the A& P to get the traditional snowstorm items: milk, bread, cigarettes for Kenny. She laughed to herself that they had plenty of toilet paper at home. Though the parking lot had only a sprinkling of vehicles, they were scattered about haphazardly to avoid the piles of plowed snow that sat like miniature mountains. Exhaust, from the multitude of vehicles turned them into ugly black mounds.

A grocery bag in one arm, keys in hand, Katie threaded her way through the slush back to her car. As she unlocked the door a quick movement caught her eye. She glanced up and saw a car entering into the parking lane she stood in. Making the turn too fast it fish-tailed, then righted. Although the car wore remnants of snow on the roof and the trunk, Katie could see a shiny blue hood coming her way. Thinking it might be Kenny she raised one hand to wave. Swerving again, it seemed to hone in on her. Katie turned her head away to avoid slush from splashing in her face. She jumped to keep from being hit. The blue car continued on.

With such a quick, awkward leap, she landed on a chunk of ice and twisted her ankle. She felt as though she floated to the ground. The paper bag split down the side and her groceries scattered. Her leg crumbled beneath her with a sickening crack. Intense pain began at the ankle and spread through her entire body with the heat and sharp sparks of July fourth fireworks. Dimly aware that her leg had broken, she was unconscious before she hit the frozen pavement.

Someone dialed 9-1-1. Within minutes an ambulance pulled up beside Katie, having been directed by one of the people from the crowd who had gathered to help. She regained consciousness before the rescue team stood nearby. When asked which car belonged to her, she pointed. The door stood open, and one of the women nearby collected Katie's groceries, placed them on the back seat, then pushed the locking-buttons down and closed the doors.

"Thanks," Katie whispered.

Her handbag still hung from her arm. She pulled the strap up onto her shoulder and tried to put a brave smile on her face as the attendants loaded her onto a stretcher and into the rear of the ambulance. The emergency signal light on the roof winked red as the driver was given the go-ahead to exit the parking lot. Not being a life-or-death situation, no siren blared.

Once on the main road they picked up a little speed. Thanks to the plow crews, most of the snow that had covered the streets now filled a long row along the curb although it blocked an area one lane of traffic would normally use. The pavement showed remnants of the sand and salt used to melt the snow and aid with traction. Progress continued uneventfully to the hospital. Katie tried to ignore the pain and concentrate on what had just happened. *I can't believe it. I'm in an ambulance headed for the hospital. My damned leg is broken. I just know it is. How did this happen? Man, this leg hurts. HURTS! Gotta be brave. I'm no sissy-baby. Someone will help soon; we must be almost there.*

Since she was conscious they wheeled Katie to the registration desk in the Emergency Room to take care of paper work. "Is there family, or anyone you'd like us to call?" The woman behind the desk asked.

"Yes," said Katie. "Please call my husband." She gave their phone number.

With every breath the pain increased. She gasped. Holding back tears became an effort. Once checked in, and placed in a waiting room, an orderly helped her into a wheelchair that kept her leg elevated and propped out toward the front. He pushed the chair into an area where she could change clothes to have an x-ray taken. Katie tried to pull her jeans off without even thinking about taking her boots off first. Although knowing she'd have to start again, she ached all over and couldn't manage to get the job done. Katie called for a nurse who came and removed Katie's boots for her, then used a pair of scissors and cut the jeans up the outer seam of the leg that had been hurt. She helped her slip into a hospital gown, and then onto a gurney. After covering Katie's lower half with a sheet they rolled into the radiology area.

The x-rays completed, Katie was taken into a room and lifted onto a bed. They packed ice bags around the leg to keep the swelling to a minimum. Shivering, trying to blink back tears, she'd never felt pain like this. With no idea what to expect, all she could do was wait. She closed her eyes. Thoughts that drifted back to several hours earlier made her wonder whether she had been careful enough. *But, accidents do happen. Every day. The newspapers are full of stories just like this one.*

Flowing in and out of reality for the next few hours produced fuzzy images of a crowd of people; alternating sensations of cold and warmth; unfamiliar faces; and unbearable discomfort. Slivers of sharp, hot pain shot in all directions through her leg whether or not she tried to move.

Hoping they'd kept their word to call Kenny, she wished he'd get there soon. Being alone, and in such agony, she wanted his arms around her telling her he'd take care of her.

That everything would be all right.

CHAPTER TWENTY-ONE

"Are you in a lot of pain?"

Katie turned her head to see a nurse standing by her bed.

"Yes, it really hurts. And I can't move my leg at all."

"I can give you a shot to make you more comfortable."

"That would be great. I need something. The longer this goes on the tougher it gets. I'm running out of being brave."

"Okay, a shot it is." She turned back the sleeve of the hospital gown Katie wore, produced a syringe, swabbed Katie's arm with alcohol and swiftly injected the drug. "That should help."

"I hope so." Katie asked, "Now what? What will they do?"

"Dr. Saxon is looking at your x-rays now. He'll decide whether you need surgery or if the break will heal properly with only a cast. He should be in to see you before too long. You must have taken quite a tumble."

"Yeah, I did. Some stupid driver came down the lane too fast, slid on the icy pavement, and damned near hit me. I had to jump to get out of the way. When I landed I stepped on something hard, lumpy. Maybe a chunk of ice, I don't know for sure, but I twisted my ankle and down I went. Everything after that is pretty much a blur."

"Timing is really bad. Holidays right around the corner. I'm sure you don't want to spend much time here in the hospital."

"No, I don't. I've never been a patient in a hospital before, but already I'm not thrilled with being here. It's not your fault—I don't mean to whine, but I hurt and I'm really getting grouchy.

And I want to go home."

"Try to get some rest if you can. Dr. Saxon will be in pretty soon and he'll give you a better idea of what's going to happen."

"Do you know if anyone has called Kenny, my husband? Someone said they'd give him a call. Just to see him now would make me feel better."

"I don't know, but I'll check. If there's anything to tell, I'll come back and let you know. Meanwhile, rest the best you can and wait for the doctor."

"Okay, thanks. I'll try."

The medicine in the shot began to take effect. As the pain lessened, Katie's mind returned again to what had happened. She worked at trying to sort it out, but none of it made any sense. So now, here she was, waiting. Just waiting. Waiting for Kenny to come. Waiting for the doctor to tell her what had to be done to get her back into shape. Waiting to go home.

Certainly Kenny will come as soon as they call him. He's not a worrier, but he does look out for me. He'll be here soon.

CHAPTER TWENTY-TWO

Exhaustion captured her She closed her eyes and wished for a nap.

"Katie?" A male voice roused her.

Not sure whether she'd slept, she turned her head to the sound. "Yes?"

"I'm Dr. Saxon." He extended his hand. "Can you tell me what happened?"

Katie relayed the details again, hoping she wouldn't need to repeat it to someone else, too.

"How are you feeling right now? You do have a break. Are you in a lot of pain?"

"It hurt so much at first I could hardly stand it. Someone put ice packs around my leg. They said it was to keep the swelling down. I think the ice made my leg numb and because of that I couldn't feel much pain for quite a while.

"Later, it started up again. A nurse came in and asked if I wanted a shot to ease the pain. The answer was a big 'yes'."

"Did the shot help?"

"It did. I think I may have dozed off for a few minutes afterward. Now, I'm totally wiped out."

"Well, the good news is that you won't have to stay here a long time. Better news is that you only need a cast, no surgery."

"Oh, a cast? Yeah, I guess that makes sense. But I can go home today, can't I? This place is not exactly Disney World."

"Well, today is over. It's already tonight." He looked at his watch. "It's nearly eight thirty. And yes, you should be able to go home tonight if you have someone to take you there."

"I'm sure my husband will be here soon. He wasn't with me and doesn't know about the accident. The woman where I checked in said she'd give him a call. Then he'll come and take me home."

"Okay, someone will be in and get you ready to have the cast put in place. If all goes well we'll have it done in an hour or so."

Two hours went by and Katie, her leg in a cast from ankle to below knee, waited in the hospital bed wishing Kenny would hurry up. Aggravated at him for not being there already she buzzed for a nurse.

"Is it all right if I use the phone here on the night table?" Katie asked. "Can I simply call an outside line or do I need to dial some other number, a nine or something, first?"

"Sure," the nurse told her. "Just go ahead and dial like you would at home. Do you need some help?"

Katie squirmed around in the bed and found that, with a little difficulty, she could sit up. "I'll be fine," she said. "Thanks."

She dialed. It rang six times without an answer. Maybe someone had already called him and he was on the way. Replacing the receiver she decided she'd wait a few minutes and then try again just to be sure. The third ring produced Kenny's voice in an irritated "hullo".

"Ohh, Kenny," she sobbed. "It's Katie."

"Well, where the hell are ya? Do ya have any idea what time it is? That's some grocery-shopping trip ya took. Ya been gone five hours. What the hell did ya buy that took five freakin' hours?"

Stunned, Katie had no words.

"Katie! Ya there? Answer me!"

She choked down angry tears. "Yes, Kenny, I'm here. I'm in room 203 at Holy Cross Hospital."

"Whatcha doing there?"

"I have a broken leg. They brought me here in an ambulance."

"Well, now, ain't that just grand."

"Someone here at the hospital said she'd call you and let you know about the accident and ask you to come and drive me home."

"Yeah, well ain't no one called here. And it's damn near midnight. Whatcha *really* been up to?"

This time, she swallowed down white-hot fury. "Kenny, dammit, *Kenny* listen to me! My car is still on the A & P parking lot. And I can't drive anyway. My leg's in a cast. I need to come home. Can you come and get me or not?"

"Sure thing, Kates, I'll be there in a few." Click.

Enough. For the first time since this incident occurred, Katie cried. Really cried. She bawled like a baby. This seemed so crazy.

CHAPTER TWENTY-THREE

The nurse walked in to check on her. "Hey, don't cry. Things will be better soon. I checked with Mary at the registration desk. She told me they finally got hold of your husband and told him what had happened. He's probably on the way by now. So try to cheer up."

These pieces were from different puzzles. They didn't fit together at all.

* * *

The nurse came back to Katie carrying a plastic bag emblazoned with the hospital's logo. Inside were the clothes she'd been wearing when she came in. Someone had cut one leg off her jeans and now the nurse helped her dress with the good leg protected by denim, the broken one heavy with a cast. Katie sat in a wheelchair tired, angry, and confused, and counting on Kenny to arrive soon.

* * *

Kenny, an ugly expression his face, followed an attendant in to see Katie. His surly behavior did not have a positive effect on the nurse. The suggestion that he go back to the parking area and bring his car to the hospital entrance caught his attention. She'd bring Katie down in the elevator and outside to the car. He should apply a smile to his lips and be ready to take her home.

He stared at Katie, obviously expecting some sort of explanation. Katie glared at him. The tension was so strong it seemed to make the air crackle.

"Right. See ya out front," he said. He turned on his heel and left.

Getting into the car proved a difficult task, but with a little help she managed. As they pulled out of the parking lot, Katie stared at the road. It glistened with a new thin coat of ice now that the sun had been asleep for several hours and chilly air had made the temperature drop. A cold, dark night greeted her through the windshield.

Neither spoke. The smell of beer and a cloud of Marlboro smoke assaulted her senses. Tucking it into memory for later, she knew better than to comment on it now. Adjusting her position in the seat as best she could, she thought she should keep an eye on Kenny hoping it wouldn't be obvious. He looked straight ahead, almost as if in a trance. He gripped the steering wheel with all his might as though the car might take off and fly if he relaxed his hold.

"*What*?" he yelled, turning his head toward her. He'd caught her staring at him.

"Just changing position," she bluffed. "You doing okay?"

He answered with action: drive faster; darkness and icy road be damned.

"Kenny, take it easy, will you?"

"Ya wanna go home? Ya wanna go home? We're fuckin' goin' home!"

She couldn't tell if he was drunk or sober, mad or crazy. But she knew *she* was scared.

Less than a mile to go now. Not bothering to slow, he turned the corner. The car fish-tailed, knocking over a trashcan someone had left at the curb. Without so much as a slight pause, he continued on. Where had she seen that happen before? Katie sucked in her breath and gritted her teeth to keep from saying something she'd regret. *Just be glad that was a trashcan and not a car or a person.*

"Oops, baby," said Kenny. "We'll get there one way or the other." He glanced at her, his look menacing, testing.

"I know we will."

A few minutes later he yanked the steering wheel to the right, whipping the car into their driveway. Stopping bare inches from the garage, he pulled the key from the ignition and got out slamming the door behind him. The jolt sent snow sliding in little patches off the car roof and onto the ground.

It looked like he would go into the house and leave her to fend for herself. She opened the door on her side, hoping to catch him.

"Kenny," she called out, "will you help me here? I don't think I can get out of the car without leaning on you. And I definitely need help getting into the house."

"Oh, yeah, sure." He came to her side of the car.

"Here, Kates," he said, reaching out to her. "Put yer arms around my neck and I'll get ya out of there and inside where it's warm."

What? WHAT? Is this the same man she'd called from the hospital? The same man who'd driven her home? Was she going crazy?

Once in the house, Katie decided not to rattle Kenny's cage. The questions burning in her head would have to go unasked. For now. Things were peaceful at the moment. Physically and mentally spent, she had no energy left to argue. Maybe he'd just been worried and reacted badly.

He helped her off with her clothes and slip into an old-fashioned flannel nightgown she kept for the coldest nights. Suggesting she might be more comfortable alone in the bed he volunteered to sleep in another bedroom. Relieved, she agreed wholeheartedly. He tucked her in and lightly kissed her forehead.

""'Night, Kates," he said. "Tomorrow I'll go get the crutches they said yer gonna need."

Fitful sleep, interrupted by extreme discomfort that gave way to flashbacks of recent events, produced a miserable scenario in Katie's mind. Trying to move forward, it occurred to her she'd need to call the school and let them know she'd be out for a few weeks. *What a great way to begin a new job! I've been there barely three months. Well, Christmas break will be here soon, I can go back to work right after that. I won't be missing so much time after all.* She forced the thoughts away, concentrating on the need to get some rest. Believing she'd be able to think more clearly and rationally in the morning, she finally drifted off.

CHAPTER TWENTY-FOUR

Usually an early riser, today broke the pattern. The glowing blue numbers on the digital clock flipped from eight-fifty-nine to nine just as she turned over to check the time. The aroma of fresh coffee wafted through the air. A wonderful morning smell. Comforting. Normal. Sitting up in bed she surveyed the room, mentally establishing a route to the kitchen. She would need to hold onto something every step of the way and put the least amount of pressure as possible on the leg. That would be a challenge. But first, she really needed to pee.

Not able to stand without assistance she worked her way off the bed and slid onto the floor. Although she could bend her knee, she sat, keeping the cast straight out, and managed to scoot along pushing with the good leg and both arms. She'd had quite a workout by the time she reached the bathroom. Afterward, floundering along the hall floor like a new kitten, she headed toward the kitchen.

"Mornin', Kates. How ya feelin'? Need a little help there?" Kenny appeared and stood in front of her, arms outstretched.

"Yes, thanks." She raised her arms to him. "The coffee smells great. I could really use a cup. Thanks for making it."

He helped her off the floor and onto a chair by the table, then poured a cup of coffee for her. Thoughts of last night bounced in her head like lightening bugs in a lidded jar. She felt an urgent need to tell him details of the accident, as best she could recall, and explain how none of it had been her fault–just one of those things. That might clear the air and maybe he'd be able to offer a reason for his own behavior. *He's used to me being home on time. Since it was so late, he probably worried. On top of that I was hurt and in the hospital. Those things might have sparked his anger and anxiousness.*

Today began on an up-note, and though that might not be the complete reason why, she decided another time might be better for such a conversation. She let it go.

CHAPTER TWENTY-FIVE

Elwood drove Kenny to the A & P parking lot to retrieve Katie's Pinto. The split bag, loosely wrapped around a loaf of bread, a container of milk and a carton of Marlboros, still lay in the back seat. True to his word, on the way home, Kenny stopped at a medical supply store and bought crutches for her, even remembering to get directions on how to adjust the to the patient's height. The slow healing process began.

By the time Katie had mastered the crutches the next appointment with Dr. Saxon was only a day away. Two weeks had melted along with the snow.

"Katie," said Dr. Saxon. "The cast needs several more weeks."

"Oh, you can't take it off?"

"No, not yet. But, I'll attach a metal bar to the bottom of it for support. You'll be able to walk short distances without crutches, providing it's comfortable."

"That's a little better, I guess. Those crutches still give my armpits a fit."

"To be on the safe side I'd suggest you lean on a cane the first day or two. Be sure to remember to hold it in the hand opposite the cast. You'll need to do that for proper balance. If this proves successful, the cast might be removed before Christmas."

* * *

Because Kenny couldn't take another day off work, Susan drove Katie to the follow-up appointment with Dr. Saxon. He believed it needed ten more days before the leg was strong enough to be dependable for her to ease back into her ordinary life. So the cast would remain in place till after the holiday.

That same night, on his way home from work, Kenny stopped at a Christmas tree lot. There were dozens to choose from now that the holidays begged for attention. Finding a suitable table-top-sized tree he bought it, stuffed it into the trunk of his car and headed home. He carried it inside and plopped it on the kitchen floor.

"Lookie here, Kates, I gotcha a Christmas tree! Ya can set it right on a table and won't have to do a lot of work fixin' it up 'cause it's just a little thing."

"Great idea, Kenny. Thanks."

"You ain't happy 'bout it?" The question sounded edgy, almost challenging.

"I am, Kenny. Truly I am." She smiled at him and refused to rise to the bait. "But we'll need to get some sort of stand to hold it. And we have nothing to decorate it with." She smiled again, "Want to take me shopping?"

"Now? Aw, geez. No, not now."

"Well, tomorrow will be fine. We'll need some things sooner or later anyway. Now that we have a tree, we may as well get them sooner. Christmas is almost here."

"Yeah, well, I have something going on with the guys tomorrow. There's a huge car show at the fair grounds. Ya think Susan could drive ya around?"

"Maybe. I'll give her a call. She likes to go shopping, so this would be a chance to look for something different and have some fun."

"I'll make a deal with you," said Susan.

"Oh, what kind of a deal?"

"Well, I have some errands to run tomorrow morning. If you let me buy lunch, I'll pick you up about twelve-thirty. We'll splurge on a great meal and then shop till we drop. I could use a few new ornaments for our little tree as well. There are some really pretty ones out there this year."

"Sounds good to me. I haven't been to the mall since before…uh…for a while. Christmas will have come and gone if I don't get busy. Starting with a good lunch we should have plenty of energy."

"Great! I've barely seen you since the accident. We need to catch up," said Susan.

That was true. After the accident most of their conversations had been short and on the phone, not in person. And, though Katie had told her what she remembered happening, she neglected to mention the blue car that had caused her to jump.

"Okay, I'll be looking for you."

CHAPTER TWENTY-SIX

They headed to Barnaby's, one of their favorite casual restaurants. Looking over the menu, Katie laid it aside. "What are you going to eat?"

"Are you kidding? You know they have the best cheese-steak subs anywhere. I can't even think about getting anything else."

They ordered. Talk slowed while they enjoyed one of their favorite sandwiches. Afterward, although not yet traditional cocktail hour, a mixed drink appealed to them both They sat sipping and talking until they realized they'd better get going before it got too late and their mission got pushed from memory.

Katie, hobbled along, trying to keep up with Susan as they toured the mall. With Christmas sales in full bloom, they found bargain after bargain and loaded up on decorations and a few small presents for their 'significant other'. Arriving back at Katie's, Susan helped her in with the shopping bags. Kenny and the guys hadn't returned from the car show yet.

"Sit a while," Katie said. "I'll put coffee on."

"Good, it'll be nice to relax. The way we walked, I felt like we were training for a race. And it's really freezing outside. A cup of coffee would be perfect right about now."

Katie got the pot going then began to sort through the bags, spreading out the contents on the kitchen counter.

"How about helping me put this little tree into the stand?" asked Katie.

"Sure," answered Susan. "It's not as small as you described. Looks like it might be a little over three feet tall. Once it's in the stand the rest will be easy, and more fun."

Between the two of them they made sure the tree was secured and sturdy. Susan helped Katie unfolded a card table in the corner and covered it with a red tablecloth. Together they lifted the tree up and placed it in the center of the table.

"It looks better already," said Susan.

"It does. Before we start decorating, I'd better pour some water into the base. You've got to keep a live tree green. When they dry out they turn into a fire hazard. It could happen. As much as Kenny is smoking these days a spark from one of his damned cigarettes might be all that's needed. Poof–up it goes!"

"Isn't he thinking about quitting?"

"Yeah, right. Like that's going to happen. He talks a good game. The man has no common sense and less self control."

"Wow. Do I hear a little bitterness there?"

"I guess you do. His lousy reaction to this accident in general, and my broken leg, and a few other things still stick me like a needle. I'll get past it. It'll just take some time."

"Well, maybe with the holidays, and then getting your cast taken off, you can start fresh with the new year."

"Ahh, I hope so. He's just so up and down. Impossible to predict from one day to the next. I'm sure part of it's me. Once I go back to work I'll feel more useful. That will make me happier. I truly love my job and this leg has me totally bummed out."

"You've managed pretty well, I think," said Susan.

"Maybe, but there have been so many changes because of it. There are a lot of things I can't do, or need help with. And no sex the whole time. Oops! Didn't mean to blurt that out. Sorry."

"Why?"

"Why what? Why I didn't mean to blurt it out? Or why no sex?"

"Might as well go for both."

"At first the leg hurt too badly to give sex much thought. The damned cast is so heavy that even when the leg didn't hurt all the time I couldn't move very well. You know, um, participate. You know what I mean."

"Yeah, I do. It just sounds major coming from you. You're the one who wouldn't talk about it. Remember?"

"Not a lot has changed there. That was a slip-up. I'm still not eager to talk about it."

Conversation trickled to a halt as they concentrated on making the little tree happy with twinkling lights and glittering decorations.

"Looks pretty good, don't you think?" asked Katie.

"It does," agreed Susan. "Now, I think it's time for me to get my butt home. Joe will wonder if I broke *my* leg." She laughed. "We'll finish that other part of the conversation later."

"Okay. Well, thanks so much. You're such a terrific friend. I really don't know what I'd do without you." She hugged Susan. "I truly love you."

"Now, don't go getting all mushy on me," said Susan. "We've been friends since grade school. Close to twenty years. We've always had each other's back. That's not likely to change. But, I love you, too."

"Good to know," said Katie.

* * *

A low-key holiday fit perfectly with their moods. Katie and Kenny exchanged a few small gifts and relaxed on Christmas day. Elwood phoned, then came by bringing a huge basket of assorted fresh fruit. A shopping bag in his other hand held a take-out dinner from The Golden Flame, a nice steak place.

"Merry Christmas," he bellowed. "Ho, ho, ho! Katie, you'll need to toss this in the oven for a while. You know, heat it up. But here's dinner for us tonight."

"Thanks, Elwood. How nice. That's very thoughtful."

"You're welcome, for sure. Sorta pay-back for some of the times I've mooched off you two." He hugged her and gave a light kiss on the cheek.

As Katie cleaned up after the meal, Kenny and Elwood sat near the tree chugging one beer after another enjoying an after-dinner glow.

An hour later the three of them sat in the living room talking about many of the changes this year brought. Some good, some not. They agreed that the next year should be a better one, and moving on with good intentions and positive thoughts would be the best way to begin. Before long, both men sat like slugs, slouched down on the sofa, lost in some world unknown to others.

"Bedtime, guys," Katie announced. "Merry Christmas."

CHAPTER TWENTY-SEVEN

Katie worried that she might not have a job to go back to after being off more than a month. Though relieved that a series of substitute teachers had handled her class during her absence, she was eager to re-establish her position. She'd missed the kids. They'd missed her, too.

From the start she'd become attached to the children. In return, they seemed to look on her with something barely short of awe. They'd argue about who would sit beside her in reading circle.

One day Katie held up a chart. "Okay, kids, I've made a poster. This column lists the name of each of you. They're in alphabetical order, so no one can complain. The next column shows a day of the week. Each person will match the day by her name. That's her day to sit by me during reading circle. Everyone gets a fair turn."

Problem solved. Satisfaction all around.

It felt good to be back. In addition to being delighted with her students, the school staff, being friendly and cooperative, furthered Katie's peace of mind that she'd chosen the right profession. The common goal was to educate the kids and, in some cases, the parents as well. Everyone needed to be aware of school rules, grading methods, acceptable behavior for both parents and students. That's how they believed a successful program worked best.

Almost daily evidence of time well spent was shown in the student's knowledge and behavior. It buoyed Katie's confidence and prompted her to remember again how important a good teacher could be. She contributed by encouraging them to want to learn. They found it exciting. The excitement transferred to Katie ten-fold. Thinking back again of how she'd adored her own teachers, she felt happy and proud now to join their ranks, hoping that someday, when these kids grew up, they'd remember her with similar fondness.

It seemed impossible that in a few short weeks she'd be handing out final report cards for this class. School would be ending the middle of June. This was the last week of May. She'd made it through the first year. A happy, fulfilling year.

* * *

Although summer vacation had barely begun, Katie felt a void. She missed the kids and how their happy faces greeted her each morning. Used to going to work every weekday, she actually missed that, too.

At home, keeping the house clean took a few hours a day at most. That left hours, empty hours, for her to use as she chose. Boredom began to work its way in.

The summer weather agreed with her, so doing a little yard work and planting a few flowers kept her interested and busy for a while. Still, that didn't take up much of the time she had to kill. She'd never really had a hobby. The closest would be reading a good book. Re-igniting that passion, parts of many days were now spent sitting on the porch reading and sipping a glass of iced tea. Sliding into a new comfort area, before long she decided life was good.

* * *

One Monday, as she began doing the laundry, using the old wringer washing machine, again, jangled her nerves. Since she'd already started, she continued until it was done. Although not minding hard work, this seemed unnecessary in today's modern times. Throughout winter she'd hung the wash in the basement. That turned out to be a nightmare. Especially rough were the weeks that the cast was on her leg. Months later, a springtime rain-shower forced her to run to the yard and grab clothes off the lines. Those memories cemented her resolve. *Laundry takes entirely too much time. This is the last day I waste hours babysitting dirty clothes.*

The next morning she hopped into her little Pinto and drove to Sears. Returning home a few hours later she had paperwork, receipts, delivery and installation arrangements made for a brand new Kenmore automatic washer and an electric dryer. Her thrill went beyond that: they would remove the old washer when they delivered the new appliances.

She decided to hold off telling Kenny. Although not positive he'd be okay with it, she felt confident that once the appliances had been delivered he wouldn't raise a fuss. They could easily afford it, but he often resented her making a decision without his approval.

Well, it's done, and that's that. I've talked to him about it before with only vague replies. Never said no, never said yes. By god, I can make a decision on my own. And once he sees what a time-saver it is he'll wonder why we didn't do it sooner.

Katie felt liberated.

The joke turned out to be on her. The old washing machine had been hauled away along with all the packing materials of the delivered equipment. The new washer and dryer, installed in the basement, had been used twice before Kenny had a clue they were there.

He'd gone to the basement to put a case of beer in the extra refrigerator. When he saw the two shiny white machines sitting there, proud as can be, he yelled up the stairs, "Kates, where'd these new laundry things come from?"

Maintaining complete control, Katie called down, "Sears."

"Yeah," he laughed. "**_Ken_**more. My namesake. Get it? Good choice."

Not offering more and expecting an argument, she had prepared to defend the purchase. There was no need. For some reason, he never mentioned it again.

* * *

Routine seldom altered. Kenny left for work early every morning. Katie took care of household chores, grocery shopping and met Susan for lunch once or twice a week. Elwood stopped by at least two evenings a week. He and Kenny would often get lost in talk that, not only didn't include Katie, but bored her. Letting them have guy-time she'd go sit on the screened porch and read or get involved in plans for classes when summer was over and she went back to teaching.

Next summer I'll get a temporary job while school is out. The days are just dragging now. Maybe I should quit teaching and get a full-time, year-round job doing something else. I'm used to being busy. Now with no real goals, nothing's going on. The business courses I took at Maryland will come in handy. Even though I have no actual work experience in the business field I'm sure, with a little training, I could be valuable to some company. Next spring I'll start reading the employment section of the want-ads. I'll check with Susan. Maybe she'll have some suggestions. This time next year I should have a new job.

CHAPTER TWENTY-EIGHT

With the bright summer sun begging her to come out and play, Katie thought about the two of them heading to the beach for a few days. It took only a moment for the disastrous memory of their honeymoon in Ocean City to sneak its way into her head. Not wanting a repeat of that event, she chose her words carefully when she mentioned the idea to Kenny.

"Well, Kates, ya know I really gotta work."

"Kenny, we could go for a weekend. What do you think about that? Just a couple of days."

"I dunno. Remember last time we went to OC? I burned to a crisp. Not sure I wanna try that again. Laying out in the sun like that is hot and boring anyway."

No mention of the huge argument/stand-off that had lasted for days afterward.

* * *

Still, the beach called. She and Susan talked about it. Joe, (now Susan's husband), would be out of town on business the end of July. He had a buddy who owned several condos at the beach. Joe would check with him and see if one might be available for Susan and Katie to use. He agreed it would be good for the two best friends to spend a week or so at the beach. The two of them thought it was a great idea, too. They needed to come up with a plan. Of course, Katie would have to figure a way to keep Kenny from being completely pissed off that she'd take a trip without him.

"Kenny," she started. "Susan and I have been thinking about giving you guys a break from the two of us."

"Yeah? How ya gonna do that?"

"Well, we really like the beach, and you two don't. Joe will be out of town on a business trip the end of July. That will leave Susan alone with not much to do but her job. She has some vacation time coming. So we've decided to take a few days away and go to Ocean City. You and Elwood could just be *guys* here around the house while we're gone. Watch whatever you want on TV, eat whenever you feel like it. Do stuff to your car. Go to bed when you're tired. No one to tell you what to do. No nagging."

" So what's tha' catch?"

"We'll be back."

Kenny laughed at that, surprising Katie. "Hey, ya' got a deal."

"Really? *Really*, Kenny? You don't mind? Oh, thanks! We we're hoping you'd be okay with it. It'll be such fun to spend some time together without thinking we need to be home in an hour or two. Girl talk and all that. Thanks, this is great." She hugged him and kissed his cheek. He beamed as though he'd just won five-hundred bucks on a lotto ticket.

* * *

Susan's car, being newer than Katie's, would be their transportation. They agreed to split gas costs, and maybe share driving as well. She pulled up at their house to get Katie just as Kenny left for work. He breezed out, wishing them a lot of fun on their 'little vacation'.

Katie loaded her suitcase into the trunk, then hoisted a cooler onto the back seat. She'd filled it with sodas and sandwiches to eat along the way. A bag with chips and cookies was propped up next to it. No need to waste time stopping for lunch. Keep moving and get to the beach. They'd relax there and feast on seafood for a week. No husbands. No noise. Peace.

The Maryland drive from Silver Spring to Ocean City took about three-and-a-half hours. It felt like less as they chattered the entire way.

"So, this friend of Joe's is a guy who owns the condo?" asked Katie.

"Yeah, he is. He's in real estate and has been lucky with some of the deals he's made. So he actually owns a few, in several different buildings. Renting them out works well for him. They stay occupied nearly year 'round. I'm amazed at the number of people who like to spend part of a winter there at the beach. The temperature goes below freezing often and if you can't walk along the shore in comfort, what's the point? It seems like he always keeps one unoccupied for his own use, or if he has a friend in need."

"Well, I'm excited about being by the ocean again. My last time there was not much of a vacation."

"How did you manage to convince Kenny to let you go? That couldn't have been easy."

"Let me go? He's not my boss, I don't have to have his permission."

"Well, yeah, true enough. But he does try to control you."

"You know, Susan, I think you're right. That's something I keep trying to figure out. He's a piece of work. I've got to choose every word so carefully that it's driving me nuts. He can twist something I say into some meaning that suits his mood du jour. How do you handle that with Joe? He seems way more easy-going than Kenny is."

"Joe and Kenny are completely different types. Joe likes to talk things out. He's not perfect, but we rarely argue. He's willing to take a close look at both sides. I guess he gets that from being a lawyer."

"It'd be nice if Kenny could get into that frame of mind. He does have his good moments. But his temper is awful. Honest to god, he explodes over something that I think is nothing. And there's no warning of what's coming. Or when. No one told me that marriage could be anything like this. I'm never prepared to do battle. I can't remember hearing a single argument between my parents."

Conversation stopped. Each of them flowed into thoughts of solutions to the problems in Katie and Kenny's marriage.

* * *

The Chesapeake Bay Bridge stretched out in front of them. Katie dug into her purse taking out money for the toll to drive over the bridge. Handing it to Susan she said, "Pull over to the side when we get across. I'll drive the rest of the way if you want me to."

"No, thanks. I'm doing fine. This is an easy trip. And thanks for funding the toll. We're nearly there now."

"This time there won't be any pressure. I'm going to enjoy it!"

"Me, too. I've been looking forward to this since the day we started talking about it."

"We'll probably gain ten pounds apiece while we're here. I love Phillips Seafood, and there are a ton of other good restaurants. You can count on me eating a real breakfast here. At home I'll have a cup of coffee, and a muffin or a piece of toast.

On the weekend I'll fix some eggs and bacon. That's a real treat. Kenny likes that, and so do I. But now, even though I won't be in a hurry, I won't have to fix a thing. We can have a big breakfast at a restaurant if we want to. They'll serve us."

"I'm sure we'll fix some meals in," said Susan. "He said this place has a nice kitchen. We can eat on the balcony and watch the waves if we feel like it."

"Yeah, even better. That will be terrific. We'll be there soon. I can hardly wait."

* * *

Directions being perfect, by noon they pulled into the parking space for the condo. Dragging their suitcases behind them, they trudged to the elevator and pushed the button for the seventh floor. Susan took the key from her pocket and unlocked the heavy metal door. Once inside they felt as though they had stepped into another world. Clean and bright, with attractive artwork on the walls, it was lovely.

"So, this is how the other side lives," said Katie. "Wow, it's totally beautiful."

"It is," agreed Susan. "Everything looks brand new. Modern. Perfect. What a place we've fallen into! Let's unpack and check out the beach for a while before dinner."

* * *

The days zipped by: tanning on beach towels by the ocean; splashing in the private pool for condo residents; eating steamed crabs, grouper, crab cakes, corn on the cob, baked potatoes, salads and slaws. Predictably, breakfasts stayed low-key, and in the condo. Usually coffee, cereal and a piece of fruit. Often they ignored lunch. The tummy can hold only so much.

After giving some thought to going night-clubbing, they decided it would be more relaxing to stay in and read, or maybe play a game of cards. A television stood in the living area if they needed a diversion or wanted to catch up on the daily news.

"Guess we're just two old married ladies," Susan laughed.

"Well, for me, beach vacations are for good food and relaxing, not for being wild and crazy. Guess I've outgrown that urge."

* * *

As they packed up and prepared to leave for home, Katie had a rush of emotion remembering the honeymoon disaster. She turned to Susan, "You know, this is the way it should have been when Kenny and I were here. Why didn't it work out?"

"I don't have an answer for you. The two of you are such an unlikely match." Susan paused before continuing with carefully chosen words. " Both of you have changed some, but in my eyes, the change is pushing you two apart."

"Really? You see it? There is *something* not quite right. I can't put my finger on it yet. I hope I figure it out before it's too late."

"Yeah, me, too."

CHAPTER TWENTY-NINE

They pulled up in front of Katie's by three in the afternoon. Being Friday, Kenny was still at work. After unloading her things from Susan's car, and saying goodbye, Katie went in the house and started to unpack.

That done, she began tidying up and checking on how much of a mess Kenny had made. He hadn't wrecked anything, but beer cans and bottles, sitting around waiting to be disposed of, covered nearly every flat surface. She brought the re-cycle bin into the house. By the time she hauled it back to the garage it overflowed with empty containers.

If that's the worst he did, I can deal with it. I wasn't here to really live *with it. I'm sure Elwood spent a lot of time here, and maybe some of the other guys, too. Well, we all had a vacation.*

Kenny got home from work at six o'clock, as usual. "Hey, Kates, what's dinner?"

No hug. No kiss. Just another day. Like she'd never been gone.

* * *

She flipped the calendar page to August. They'd been back from the beach only a day. Still, ordinary habits fell smoothly into place. Spending the weekend getting the house back into shape and playing catch-up on the laundry kept Katie busy. She couldn't fathom Kenny's complete lack of interest about the trip she and Susan had taken. *Oh, well. I didn't spend a moment thinking about him while we were at the beach. I'm sure he's not been thinking about me. So, I guess we're even. He's been working. Susan and I were having fun.*

By Monday, as Katie continued taking care of 'wifey'

business at home, Kenny went to work. Keeping with routine, Elwood stopped by that evening as he did so often.

Thinking ahead, Katie knew, that within the week, she must fine-tune the plans for teaching her new class. Get prepared. School would start the last week of August. She'd been at home the whole week since the Ocean City trip. Now, making a list of the few more supplies she should have, pushed her into motion. Heading out to buy the needed items, she felt motivated. Happy.

Light traffic allowed her to cruise along, letting her mind dwell on the up-coming school semester. Once again excitement surfaced. With it came a flash of self-doubt. She managed to dismiss it immediately: *I've done it before and I'll do it again. I'll be fine. No first-day jitters this time. It can't get here soon enough!*

The traffic light ahead switched from green to yellow as she approached the intersection. There were no vehicles in sight. She could easily go through. But deciding to err on the side of caution she stepped on the brake pedal. Nothing happened. The car continued forward. Sailing safely through the yellow signal Katie gasped while she pushed harder on the brake. "Shit! *Shit!* Now what?"

Clicking the ignition off she sat in the driver's seat, a tight grip on the steering wheel, frightened and shaking. With both feet she put all her weight on the brake pedal, so much so that it lifted her off the seat. At last the car began to slow. She struggled to guide it into the curb where it finally came to a complete stop. Yanking on the emergency brake, she wondered why she hadn't thought of doing that right away. But she hadn't. Luckily, the car now sat still.

A glance in the rear-view mirror showed another vehicle

pulling up behind her. A man got out of his car and headed toward hers.

Not sure what to think, the decision was quickly made for her: he tapped on the window. She looked. It was a cop. As she rolled down the glass he spoke. "I saw you at the intersection, you didn't run a red, but you seemed to be having some sort of trouble. Is everything all right?"

" I'm really not sure," she said. "I put my foot on the brake and the car didn't stop. Like it had a mind of its own."

"Are you positive you stepped on the brake and not on the gas?"

That annoyed her. She'd been driving for years. "Absolutely."

"Have you had trouble with the brakes recently?"

"No. But if I had, my husband would have fixed them. He's a mechanic."

The policeman lifted the hood, and looked under the car as well. "*I'm* not a mechanic, but I can see something is leaking. Nothing's pouring out, but there is a drip. Could be brake fluid. Better have him take a look."

"Do you think it's okay for me to drive it home?"

"No. And you'll need to have it moved away from here soon. There's no parking on this street between four and seven on weekdays. Rush hour, you know. So if it's still here then, the county will tow it for you." He smiled. "That's not as a favor, you understand. It will cost you the price of the parking fine in addition to the towing fee that is more than a regular towing service would charge."

"Swell. Is there a pay phone around here anywhere?"

"None close that I can think of. I can call a tow truck for you if you like."

"Yes, please, that would be great. I certainly don't want to have an accident. And I don't want to pay a parking ticket either."

He made the call and left. She sat in her car, waiting half an hour until Tommy's Towing came to do the job. "Where do you want this towed to?" the driver asked.

She gave the name of where Kenny worked.

"And the trouble is…?"

"The brakes won't work."

"Do you know why they won't work?"

"No, I'm not at all sure. The cop said he thought brake fluid might be leaking."

"Ahh, that would do it. You don't know anyone that would mess with it do you? An angry boyfriend or something?" He laughed at his own joke. Katie didn't find it amusing.

"No, I don't. Please just tow it for me."

"Okay." He turned to leave.

Although embarrassed that she might have just sounded rude, she needed more help and called him back. "Oh, can I ask you to do me a favor?"

"What do you need?"

"Since you have a phone in your truck, will you call for a

taxi to come here and pick me up? I need to go home now, instead of shopping."

"Sure, I'll call Barwood Cab. They'll send someone. Good luck."

"Thanks."

A short time later, as a cab approached, Katie waved to let him know she would be the passenger. Reaching over the back of the front seat, the driver opened the rear door for her. She got in, giving her address. While riding home, irritation about her car surfaced. That mixed with frustration that the shopping mission had fallen apart. The supplies would have to wait. She paid the cabbie and went inside.

CHAPTER THIRTY

"Ya shoulda called *me*," Kenny complained. "I woulda towed ya for free. That jerk's charging a hundred bucks."

"How was I supposed to call you? I just got lucky that a cop saw me fly through a yellow light and stopped to be sure everything was all right."

"Sure. I'm sure that's why he stopped. He prob'ly saw a sweet young thing alone in her car and had some other ideas."

"My god, Kenny, you're nuts! He was very helpful, not at all like that. The tow truck guy was nice, too. He called a taxi for me so I could get home. Otherwise I'd probably still be hoofing it this very minute. Have you had a chance to find out what's wrong with it?"

"Yeah, looks like there's a leak in the brake fluid line. If the hose rotted I gotta replace it. I'll have it fixed by tomorrow."

"The cop said he could see something leaking, but he didn't know what. The tow truck guy said he thought it might be brake fluid."

"He's right. That's what it is."

"He also made a... um... joke. Wondered if I knew anyone who would 'mess' with it."

Kenny's head jerked to attention. He glared at her. "What did ya say to *that*?"

"Only that my husband is a mechanic and he will fix it."

"Yeah, and don't ya forget it." His chin jutted out defensively.

* * *

With the car repaired, Katie, now back in business, retrieved her list and bought supplies.

The next week, after finalizing her plans for classroom activities, she reviewed them to be sure they were satisfactory. The new semester would begin in just a few days. She would be ready. What could go wrong?

* * *

The new striped blouse felt crisp and nice across her shoulders. The navy blue skirt she chose to go with it matched perfectly. The look would be casual but professional. Stepping into the skirt and sliding it up over her hips she watched herself in the full-length mirror. The waistband felt a little tight. She had to tug to get it buttoned. *Dammit. Guess I really did go on an eating spree when we were in Ocean City. I must have put on five pounds. Maybe more. But that food is marvelous! It was worth every bite. Glad I noticed this now, though. Don't want to add to it.*

Well, it will disappear once I'm back at work. No sitting around doing nothing while I'm there. I'll be busy all day, walking through the halls, and moving around the room, checking on how the kids are doing. Taking them out to the playground. Bending, stretching…

Off to school she went, looking forward to a new crop of six-year-olds and another fulfilling semester. Passionate about her role as teacher she felt elated classes were beginning.

As she'd expected, getting back to teaching proved therapeutic. The children were a delight, the parents cooperative. She considered it a dream job. The hours were reasonable and, at

112

this grade level, she rarely had work to take home. The salary couldn't compare to other professional positions, but she doubted she'd be as satisfied doing anything else. Staying busy, now boredom had been forgotten. She looked forward to every day.

A few weeks later she realized the weight she'd put on when she and Susan were at the beach was still there. *I haven't been eating junk lately. Certainly these extra five pounds should have come off by now.* She stood on the scale in the bathroom. *Five pounds? Yikes, more. Nearly six. What was I thinking? Time to go on a diet.*

The lunch she packed for the next day consisted of only fresh veggies and a couple of pieces of fruit. No sandwich. No chips. No cookies. She decided to keep doing that for the next several weeks. Those extra pounds needed to disappear.

After weighing every morning, disappointment set in. Not an ounce had let go of her waist. *Stepping on the scale every day is a bit obsessive. I'll just do it once a week from now on.* But after another week, there showed an increase of a pound, rather than a loss. *How can that be? I've been so careful about what I eat.*

Katie's mind had been full to overflowing: the problem with the brakes on the car; then getting ready to go back to teaching; then beginning the class. Now, those things behind her, she thought about her weight and the self-imposed diet. *Maybe I should start some regular exercising.*

CHAPTER THIRTY-ONE

A week into October she had an epiphany. *Dammit! How could I have been so careless? Way back, when my leg was broken, my whole routine was shot to hell. Everything in my life turned upside down. Things gradually settled into place again and old ordinary habits were forgotten. I'm surprised I stayed lucky this long. It's been months, MONTHS, since I stopped taking the pill. Two months since I've had a period. What an idiot. I'm pregnant. We haven't talked about having a baby any time soon. I'm not positive I even want one. Now what? How can I break the news to Kenny? Who knows what he'll think? Well, I've got to be sure first. Before I mention anything to him.*

Stopping at a drug store after work the next day she bought a home pregnancy test kit. A small package, it fit easily into her shoulder bag. With each step, as she walked back to the car, the bag bumped against her hip ever so lightly. It seemed to Katie something inside the bag (the little box?) was sending out waves of heat. It felt like a volcano ready to erupt. Although knowing that was a foolish thought, she couldn't quite shake it. The need to hurry home propelled her on.

She usually got home from work before Kenny. Today proved no exception. Rushing to change from work clothes to jeans and a T-shirt kept her mind focused on normal, every-day habits. Her thoughts must be in order to follow the directions on this test to be sure of the results. Still in a light state of shock she read, then re-read, the directions. Couldn't be easier. Straddling the toilet, she peed on the little strip provided. Waiting the few minutes required, then watching in utter disbelief, she saw the strip change from cream-color to blue. Pregnancy confirmed. *Dammit! It can't be true!* She clapped one hand over her mouth to keep a scream from escaping.

Wrapped in a cocoon of her own thoughts, Katie moved like a robot while preparing dinner. The two of them sat at the table as Kenny droned on about some special, very expensive, car he was helping to rebuild. His excitement showed as he gestured with his hands, smiling and talking and laughing all the while. His happiness helped cover what Katie felt about *her* day. Feigning interest, she didn't interrupt. Rather, gave oohs and aahs at appropriate times, fortifying Kenny's desire to ramble.

Not wanting to break his bubble, she listened as he described this particular vehicle. It belonged to someone rich and famous who wanted nothing but the best. As he talked, Katie realized the machine had quickly become an obsession. She believed Kenny treated it as though *he* owned it. As though it was his baby.

* * *

Phoning Dr. Lorenzo's office the next day, Katie scheduled an appointment for Friday afternoon, three days away. Even though the pregnancy test from the drugstore had given a positive reading, she hoped there might be a mistake. She headed to the bathroom much too often, only wanting to check her panties to see if there might be evidence that her period would begin, but just be late. No such luck.

Katie flipped magazine pages, without mentally registering anything about them, as she waited for the nurse to lead her in to see Dr. Lorenzo. When someone called her name she jumped up, stumbling in her haste.

Weight, blood pressure, temperature, regular appointment tasks dispensed with, she sat in the examination room waiting for the doctor.

"Hi, Katie," he said.

Without warning she burst into tears.

"Katie, what's the trouble? Those tears surprise me."

She sniffled. "Sorry. I'm pretty sure I'm pregnant."

"And you don't want to be?"

"That I'm *not* sure of. I hadn't planned on having a baby so soon. It was a total accident. Not planned."

"What makes you think you're pregnant?"

"Well, the obvious thing: I've missed a period, maybe two. I've never kept track since I started taking the pill. I was so regular it was a no-brainer."

"So this happened with you on the pill?"

"No. After I broke my leg last winter my routine was so messed up that the only medication I ever took was for pain. I know this sounds stupid, but I truly didn't even think about taking it. And I've been regular all along. Until either August or September."

"So you've missed one or two? You're not sure which? It's entirely possible that is just a quirk. That happens now and then, and things go back to normal."

"Well, I've gained six or eight pounds *and* I took one of those home pregnancy tests. It came back positive."

"What does Kenny think about it? How does he feel?"

"I haven't told him yet."

"When do you plan to tell him?"

"Not until I know for absolute sure that I am. And, if I am, not until I've figured out what to say and how to say it."

"Katie, you know this isn't something you can hide. Start working on your plan to tell him. Time isn't on your side here. Meanwhile let's take a look, get the results from some blood work and be positive that you are pregnant. Then we can give some thought on how to approach Kenny. Especially if you think he might not be thrilled with the idea of a baby."

"Yeah, I know you're right."

Everything said and done, the diagnosis didn't change. Katie was, indeed, with child. Due sometime in April.

CHAPTER THIRTY-TWO

A dozen different methods of giving the news to Kenny danced around in Katie's head. None of them sounded reasonable. A couple seemed downright silly: she couldn't take him shopping for baby clothes; or strategically position a 'name-your-baby' book on the coffee table; or display something written by Dr. Benjamin Spock offering ideas on how to raise a child. Postponing it any longer would surely drive her nuts. She'd tell him tonight. Somehow.

When Kenny came home from work she stood at the kitchen counter putting the final touches on tonight's dinner. Coming up behind her he patted her bottom and gave it a little squeeze. "Hey, Kates, ya finally got a little meat on ya bones. Nice."

Turning to face him she blurted out, "I do, but there's a reason."

"Ya been piggin' a out a little too much?" Chuckling at the thought, he added, "Those cookies at lunchtime catchin' up to ya?"

"No. That's not it at all."

"Well, what then?"

"Kenny, uh...Kenny, I'm pregnant."

Silence billowed across the room like a gray morning fog.

CHAPTER THIRTY-THREE

Sitting at the dinner table together, neither seemed to have anything to say. Kenny clicked the television on and kept his eyes glued to it, allowing the waves of the latest news and sports reports to pour over him. He absorbed none of it.

Katie, her mind in a shambles, managed only to push food around her plate with the fork, forming little patterns and designs with the vegetables. She finally got up to clear the table. Kenny sat stone still.

"How can ya be pregnant? Ya been taking the pill."

"Well, when I broke my leg, I only took pain meds and didn't remember to take anything else. I just forgot to start taking it again when the cast was taken off and things settled down."

"Whose baby is it?" he asked with a cold, and complete lack of emotion.

"*What* did you say?"

"Who's the father?" His lips curled around the words as though he'd just tasted something very bitter.

"How in the hell can you even ask such a question?"

He stood. "I'd like to know who the sonofabitch is. Ya gonna tell me of yer own free will, or am I gonna hafta beat it outta ya?"

If she'd ever had any doubt, that was enough to convince Katie that Freon flowed through his veins.

"Kenny, you're going to be a daddy. It's your baby. How can you possibly think anything else?"

Plopping a hand on each of her shoulders, he shook her. "Who'd ya go to Ocean City with?"

"Get your damned hands off me!" She wrenched away from him, backing up and stifling the urge to slap him across the face with all her might. "I went with Susan. You know that. You were here when she came to pick me up."

"So, ya met some guy when ya was there?"

"Kenny, stop it! That's insane. You can't believe what you are saying. You know it's nothing like that. Don't be an idiot and try to make this into something it isn't."

"Yeah, well, I dunno. The timing seems about right."

"Timing be damned! It's your baby, like it or not."

"Maybe so, maybe no."

"All right, Kenny, I'm done with this. I thought you just might be happy about it. I can see that right now you aren't. You sleep on it. You think about the shit you just said to me. When you're ready to apologize let me know. Then maybe we can talk about it. Or maybe not. You want to know who the sonofabitch is? It's YOU. You are the sonofabitch!"

At that moment she changed. The feeling was both physical and mental. A sudden intellectual detachment washed over her. Screw him. And the horse he rode in on.

CHAPTER THIRTY-FOUR

The only thing that seemed to satisfy Kenny was taunting Katie. A day seldom went by without one after another of his snide remarks zinging toward her.

"So, Kates ya got nuttin' to tell me?" He'd turn and walk away without waiting to see if she'd answer. She made no comment.

As she dressed to go to work in the morning, he'd question whether she'd really be going there, or someplace else. It would be the same if she needed to make a quick trip to the grocery store. By now, pushing his ranting aside came easy for Katie. But he'd awakened a fury in her she'd had no idea existed. She almost welcomed it, feeling that it gave her extra strength to resist caving in to his bizarre behavior.

No conversation evolved, just his hateful digs. Ignoring them day and night became difficult. But she handled it: she refused to be goaded into an argument. Still, rage built up inside. With nerves frayed, she felt on edge most of the time. Finally, her anger reached an impossibly high level.

* * *

Saturday, with both of them at home all day, no relief appeared on the horizon. Kenny didn't let up. After consuming a six-pack of beer, he behaved like a nasty drunk. Slouched in his chair at the dinner table his words slurred through his lips. Picking at his food, more of it landed on the front of his shirt than in his mouth. He stared into space as if trying to make a decision on what he should do next. Placing both hands on the table he pushed so his chair would go back. Standing proved to be a chore. Once upright he remained in that position looking, for all the world, like an ancient statue beginning to crumble. A minute or two passed. A slight re-awakening directed him to the refrigerator where more beer waited for him.

Shuffling into the living room, a six-pack of Bud dangling from one finger, he flopped onto the sofa. History told her he'd pass out before long.

As she cleared the dishes she felt a consuming need to get out of the house for a while before something really awful happened. By shortly after midnight, her mind had filled with events of the past several days, she decided she needed to do something to shake off this mood. *Yes. I'll take a break. Get some fresh air. Clear my head. The way he's acting is just pissing me off. Pure rage is making my blood boil.*

She enjoyed driving. More to the point, driving fast. It exhilarated her. She might head up-county where traffic or speed never seemed to be a problem. Better yet, take a drive around the Capitol Beltway. About sixty-five miles the full distance. She could do that in an hour at this time of night. No traffic lights, a steady speed limit. Only fifty-five miles per hour, but a perfect way to burn off tension and stress. And anger.

CHAPTER THIRTY-FIVE

Swinging onto the entrance ramp at Georgia Avenue, she drove east through Silver Spring, and past College Park. All familiar territory, reminding her of daily trips to the University of Maryland several years ago. The good old days?

Pressing on the accelerator the speedometer registered sixty-three. Then sixty-seven. She went south around Landover, Capitol Heights, Morningside and into Virginia where she crossed the Potomac River near Alexandria, now heading west. Curving to the north near Spingfield, she'd driven about half-way. Still trying to empty rage out of her system she drove faster. Up to seventy now.

The circle had been completed. Slowing dramatically, she took an exit ramp back onto Georgia Avenue where she'd begun. But, now, although after two in the morning, going home held little appeal. Deciding to drive a while longer she headed north on Viers Mill Road. With virtually no traffic, but a speed limit half of what she'd been doing for the past hour, this seemed bland compared to the beltway she'd just left behind. Accelerating again she felt comfortable and in control.

Crossing Randolph Road and going down hill for half a mile a sign, that had been there for years, faced her. It read 'Reduce Speed Ahead'. Now heading immediately uphill the words on the sign seemed to be mocking her. Challenging her. She'd seen it a hundred times. *Reduce speed? Bullshit.* She pressed hard on the gas pedal.

Being familiar with the area, she knew that once she got to the top there'd be a traffic light. Believing it would be flashing yellow at this time of morning she couldn't make herself slow down.

The light glowed solid red.

She slammed on the brakes even though she saw no other vehicle anywhere, and hadn't for fifteen minutes. Her car responded by fishtailing, but stopped. For some reason having to interrupt forward progress sent her mentally over the top and into furious mode again.

Before the traffic light clicked from red to green, another light seemed to materialize out of thin air staking a claim just feet behind her. That light belonged to a motorcycle. The motorcycle belonged to the cop who rode it. He swung off the bike, strutting as he headed toward Katie. He tapped her window with his knuckles. She rolled the window down.

"Driver's license and registration, ma'm." Hands on hips. His voice gruff.

Digging into her purse she produced her license, then she retrieved the registration from the glove box.

"Do you know how fast you were driving?" This, with a holier-than-thou attitude.

That attitude didn't sit well with Katie.

"Not exactly, maybe thirty; thirty-five." *Just write the damned ticket and be on your way.*

"Do you know what the speed limit is here?"

"Yes."

"And you know you exceeded it by more than ten miles an hour?" His chest puffed out. She expected him to flex his muscles at any moment. *Pompous ass.*

"I'm not sure, but maybe."

"Are you aware that the sign, before coming up the hill, tells you to reduce speed?" His chin jutted out leaving no doubt he held the aces.

"Yes."

"Do you realize that it's unsafe to drive that fast in a residential area?" He stood taller, stiffer, more intimidating.

"Yes."

As he droned on and on about the hazards of speeding, and how badly she'd broken the law, her fury grew wild again. *Shut up and write the goddam ticket. I don't want to listen to all that. No one is on the road near here. I didn't cause a problem for anyone else. I can pay the ticket. Just don't give me a lecture.*

He opened his ticket book with a flourish. He flipped to a fresh page. As he began to write, he continued to talk. With every word he chastised her. When he finished, he held the ticket out to her.

She didn't take it.

"Sign the ticket, ma'm."

"No."

"Ma'm, I said sign the ticket."

"I'm not going to sign it."

"Ma'm, it's not an admission of guilt. It's simply stating that you have received a copy of the ticket."

She stared at him. His gaze held steady, without faltering.

His voice raised. "Sign it and give it back to me."

"No."

He dropped the ticket through the open window onto her lap.

Slowly, deliberately, she picked up the citation. Giving him one final glare, she ripped it in half. Continuing to tear it into strips, she reduced it into confetti not stopping until the entire thing had been shredded and tucked into her left hand. The entire time the cop stood there as if in a trance. Not believing what he saw.

"You want the ticket?" Katie asked. "Okay, here it is."

She extended her arm straight out the window. Palm turned down, she spread her fingers. Tiny bits of paper fluttered to the ground.

Her look challenged him. Dared him.

He matched it. She knew then, he felt he owned the power. Katie watched his eyes blaze with fury. Now, beyond backing down, she equaled it.

He broke the spell and the visual connection: "Ma'm, get out of your car and pick this up."

Katie felt empowered.

"If I pick it up, I will stuff it, piece by piece up your ass!"

Not missing a beat she put her car in gear and drove off. Checking the rear-view mirror she saw the officer standing as though glued to the spot. He seemed transfixed. Katie decided he wouldn't have been more surprised if she'd shot him.

Turning right at the first corner she headed home, stunned by her own behavior.

Her anger had been quenched only to be replaced by fear over what she'd just done. That fear lasted. And lasted. Every time the doorbell rang unexpectedly she looked out the window to be sure no policeman had come to arrest her. After all, he had whatever information might be necessary to track her down.

Strangely, he never came. The mental punishment she gave herself exceeded any he might have doled out. She never forgot it.

CHAPTER THIRTY-SIX

With no apology forthcoming, and little communication of any sort between them, brick by invisible brick, the wall keeping Katie and Kenny apart grew higher and sturdier. They continued routines as usual. Each of them headed out to work in the morning; both returned before dinner. Once at home, however, the atmosphere nose-dived dramatically. It was as though the floor had been littered with broken glass, they'd had their shoes ripped from their feet and some higher power forced them to edge around barefoot.

What little conversation slipped out, eked from between tightly closed lips with words so sharp they were painful. The rage growing inside them both festered, becoming poisonous.

* * *

The next Saturday Elwood phoned. Later he came to the house. After a while a couple of other guys ended up there, as well. The haze of summer remained, and this early November day boasted bright sunshine and warmer than usual weather.

While the men hung out in the living room, Katie chose to escape with a cup of tea and a book. She'd sit outside on the porch and read. That way she could avoid taking part in anything concerning them. She was neither their maid, waitress, nor nurse. They could damned well fend for themselves. From the kitchen, she heard the men talking in the other room. At a break in their conversation she heard Kenny speak.

"Hey, guys, guess what? I'm gonna be a daddy."

Shocked, Katie snapped to attention, needing to hear the rest of this.

"You gonna be a *daddy*?" asked Elwood. "Man, that's

somethin'."

"Yep, Katie's got a little bun in the oven. Not really planned, but what the hell, now's as good a time as any."

The men offered considerable rumbling about having a baby around, and how that would change their lifestyle.

"Yeah," said Kenny. "It sure as hell will. But ya know, it's gotta be a cute little bugger–me as the daddy–Kates as the momma."

"Can't beat that combination," one of the guys commented.

That was enough. Inner turmoil sent her to the porch, doubting she'd be able to concentrate on the book she had tucked under her arm. The overheard tidbit crawled right under her skin. Kenny certainly sounded like he was bragging. But to her face, he'd complained, questioned, challenged. Although annoyed, she felt a bit of relief that perhaps he was coming to his senses.

Still, the wedge between them grew larger. She could not predict when Kenny might explode again.

CHAPTER THIRTY-SEVEN

The pregnancy caused no disruption in Katie's activities. It turned out to be much easier than she'd thought possible. No morning sickness or any type of physical discomfort plagued her. She felt good: healthy, with a voracious appetite. No particular cravings, but a lot of whatever was available at the moment. Being padded with soft, new pounds she fairly glowed inside and out. She loved this baby already and would keep it safe and warm inside her. Once it was born, she knew her instinct would be to protect the child.

She harbored worries about how Kenny would take to having a baby around the house. He'd never spent time around little kids. In her wildest imagination, she couldn't picture him changing a diaper or reading a bedtime story to any child. And doubted he could recite the simplest nursery rhyme.

* * *

As the months moved along, Katie decided it made no sense to buy a lot of new baby clothes. Infants outgrew clothes quickly–sometimes in a matter of weeks. Now, escaping from Kenny and his friends on Saturdays, she spent a few hours driving to yard sales and thrift shops looking on for good quality baby things in great condition. Amazed at the bargains she found, she began to build a wardrobe for the child within her. Almost everything available seemed suitable for either boy or girl, making it so much easier. A bonus: while enjoying the shopping, she was bolstered by the realization it was a very smart thing to do as well. No reason to throw money away on retail prices.

After giving some thought to taking childbirth classes and learning how to breathe properly while in labor, she came to the conclusion it was silly and a waste of time. *What's the point of that? Women have been having babies since the world began. Most seemed to manage just fine without all those frills. It's natural. I'll be fine. Only a few more months to go.*

* * *

She and Kenny struggled to rebuild their shaky relationship, a tedious process overflowing with distrust and intolerance. Katie still held a grudge about what Kenny had said when she first told him she was pregnant. Apparently, he'd never even considered saying he was sorry, obviously feeling his covert acceptance of the pregnancy took the place of any imagined need for an apology.

They managed to keep their few conversations civil. Little more. It seemed they both clung to the hope that, when the baby made an appearance, all their problems would fade away. Life as they'd known it would return.

Susan made every attempt to convince Katie to dump her anger and make peace with Kenny. She wasn't a member of Kenny's fan club, but she hated the thought that if the marriage failed Katie would be devastated.

"You know, once the baby is here it will take a lot of your time. Your lives will be much more complicated. Sorry if it sounds like I'm preaching to you, but Katie, please think about what lies ahead. You are much too smart to let this grudge rule your life. If you think it won't affect the baby, think again. You need this crap to stop."

"I know. I know," said Katie. "But I'm really not sure how to go about it. He hurt me to my soul. It's harder since he won't even say he's sorry for what he said. I can't seem to bring myself to forgive him. I don't have on and off buttons to push for that. Now, every day that goes by, we're becoming more like roommates or, worse, strangers. What's more, if I give in to his stupid behavior yet again, he'll feel like he's won. Only more of the same will follow."

Katie knew the days of her innocent trust of him were over. Although wishing she could let go of Kenny's insensitive outbursts, with no reason obvious to Katie, he might go on a rampage at any moment. He sent out no warnings.

CHAPTER THIRTY-EIGHT

The end of the January and the end of the school semester were simultaneous. It also marked the end of Katie's role as teacher. The baby would be born early in April, two-and-a-half months away. She planned to spend these next few weeks turning the smallest bedroom into a nursery.

Finding a crib, a changing table, and all sort of other baby things foreign to her, filled her time. The busier she could be the better she liked it. That kept her out of Kenny's path. Conversations now centered on the weather forecast or some TV program they both might want to watch. Neutral ground.

A breakthrough came one evening as they sat before the television. Now into the eighth month, Katie regularly felt the tiny body inside her moving around. An arm, a leg, a foot – moving and causing ripples in her belly. It didn't hurt. It felt weird, but good. The wonder of it sent goose-bumps parading up her arms.

Several weeks before, the first time it had happened, she rested her hand where the action was. What excitement she felt! Something she couldn't find words to describe. Soon it became a regular occurrence and a thrill each time.

This night, the television turned onto a forgettable show, both she and Kenny sat on the sofa. Neither paid any attention to the story line, it was merely on for a diversion. Each of their minds wandered away to other thoughts. Katie rested her legs on the cushion beside her. An eye on the clock, she hoped for bedtime to come soon.

The baby was active, demanding attention. Katie placed her hand where a little mound inside her rose and fell, thus prompting a smile. Enjoying the gentle upheaval, a rush of emotion overwhelmed her.

Out of the blue, "Kenny," she whispered. "Give me your hand."

Looking at her, as if he thought she'd lost all her marbles, his first reaction was to pretend he'd heard nothing. To ignore her. He hesitated. Then, seeing the expression on her face he complied, stretching out his hand.

Katie took it, placing it on her belly. She concentrated on his face, feeling a desperate urgency to catch his expression. She had the sensation of peering through a dirty window: everything blurred together, nothing stood out sharp and clear. *Don't cry. Don't cry.*

For a reason she was not aware of, his response seemed vital to her. Kenny had not known how the baby moved inside her. Deep in a recess of Katie's mind, Kenny's reaction to feeling that, for the first time, would influence what direction their future seemed likely to go.

Beneath his hand, the force inside Katie's belly, rose and fell like a tiny wave.

"Oh, my god, Kates. That's so totally amazing. Is that the kid? Moving around in there?" He appeared to be awestruck. Happy. Proud.

"Yes. It is." Soft tears trickled down her cheeks.

He jerked his hand away. "What's the matter? Why ya cryin'? What's wrong? Is the kid all right?"

"Nothing's wrong, Kenny. The baby is fine. In your own way, you just said things are getting better. Maybe we'll be okay after all."

Could it be possible to empty her head and heart of all the mistrust and anger that had been circulating throughout the house for so many months now? A fresh start, with a new baby? Or were those things that couldn't, shouldn't be ignored? His short fuse cast constant waves of tension.

CHAPTER THIRTY-NINE

Katie flipped the calendar page to April. The ninth month. She felt heavy and clumsy. The pregnancy had been uncomplicated, and by all accounts easy. Now, so close to the end, Katie found herself wanting the process to speed up. The sooner the baby decided to emerge into the world the better.

Early on the morning of April fourteenth, contractions started. The first one, just a pain, Katie dismissed as exactly that: a pain. Then a second, third and fourth, each spaced about half an hour apart. Those would not be dismissed. This was the real deal. Kenny called the station telling them the news. He'd be taking Katie to the hospital soon instead of going to work. The baby was on its way.

Katie called Dr. Lorenzo.

"Yes, sounds like you're not too far from ready. Keep an eye on the clock. Time the frequency of the contractions. When they are every twelve to fifteen minutes give me a call back. I'll be waiting to hear from you. You live only a few minutes from the hospital. I'll meet you there."

* * *

In the labor room Katie tried to be brave. It felt like she was being ripped open. She was surprised that even her back hurt. Kenny had no idea what to say or do. He'd never seen her in such agony. The broken leg hadn't seemed to be nearly as hard on her. This was very different.

"Kates, what can I do to help?"

She rested both hands on her belly as if that would lessen the pain. Beads of sweat glistened on her brow. Reaching up to wipe them away she pushed her fingers through her hair. The dampness tangled the curls making them cling to her forehead. Another sharp pain called her hands back to where they'd just been: resting on her belly.

"Nothing, ahh…really nothing. Trouble is, that almost as soon as one pain is…ahh...over, another begins. I thought there'd be a little relief in between. Dr. Lorenzo says when they get close like this it won't be much longer. Ahh…that hurts! Sorry. Well, you go on out to the waiting room with the other dads. They'll let you know when it's over."

Thoughts of the past welled up unbidden. Needing a distraction she allowed them to continue. The arguments they'd had. The rough times. Some good times. And now this baby. And this pain! Believing that at any moment she'd cry, she remembered he had zero tolerance for her tears. She wished he'd just leave.

"Ya don't want me to stay here?"

"Ahh…while the baby is actually born?"

"Yeah."

"Do..ahh..ahh you really want to see it? Watch what's going on?"

"Uh, well, maybe not. I'm not so sure. What ya think?"

"I don't think…aah..uhh… that's a great idea. I've heard a lot of women prefer it, but not me. You go on and get some lunch or something. Ahh..uhh..you may be a daddy when you get back."

He left. She burst into tears.

Sobbing quietly as the contractions escalated, Katie finally begged for something to ease the pain.

Less than an hour later a seven-pound-four-ounce girl presented herself to the world. She squawked and squealed, louder and with more energy than you would think possible, as all newborns seem to do. Her tiny fists punched the air. Her feet kicked at nothing. The nurse weighed her, washed her off and put a diaper in place. She dressed the infant in a little open-front, long-sleeved, undershirt kind of thing that was kept closed with string ties, then covered her head with a small pink knit cap. Finally, wrapped in a baby blanket, she was given to Katie. Though thrilled, Katie felt exhausted. Joy replaced the pain that had disappeared.

Later, viewing this child through the glass window of the nursery, Kenny gasped in disbelief as the nurse held the newborn up for inspection. *That's my kid. I'm a daddy now.* After standing there for a while he went in to see Katie. As he sat on a chair beside her hospital bed, the nurse rolled a small plastic baby crib into the room. Inside, their new baby girl slept and seemed content and comfortable. Kenny nearly went into shock. He'd never been so close to such a tiny human. He was afraid to touch her. Flatly refused to hold her.

"Aw, geez, Kates, lookit what we did."

"I know. Amazing isn't it?"

"She's so small. Like a doll. A toy."

"You were that size once."

"Nah, not that little."

They fell silent letting events of the day sink in. Absorbing the enormity of it. It was one thing to be pregnant, quite a different situation to actually hold the child in your arms and think about taking care of her for the next twenty years. Daunting thoughts. Unbelievable responsibility.

Katie broke the reverie. "We need to name her before I get out of here and come home."

"Yeah, guess we do. What ya wanna call her?"

"I have a couple of ideas. Have you thought of any?"

"Nah, I prob'ly couldn't even name a goldfish. What's yer best idea?"

"My favorite is Marylee. Do you like that?"

"Sure, it's a happy name. It's fine."

Someone misspelled the name on the paperwork for the birth certificate. The error slipped through unnoticed. Marylee became Marley. Katie decided she liked that even better and wouldn't bother to have it corrected. She hadn't heard the name before and thought it had a pleasant sound besides being unusual.

Now there were three.

CHAPTER FORTY

The joy of motherhood captured Katie. Surrounded her like a soft, warm blanket. Holding Marley, feeding her from the bottle, Katie admired the tiny features. Her gaze paused on the miniature fingers: each one less than an inch long, not as big around as a pencil and ending in the slightest suggestion of a fingernail. All five fingers of one hand curled around one finger of Katie's with room to spare. The tight grip gave her extreme pleasure and amplified the need to protect this innocent, new soul. And the baby powder smell! True perfume. The best.

* * *

Kenny came home from work and saw the two of them entranced with one another. He, too, continued to feel mystified that their union had produced this small creature.

With one finger he stroked Marley's head. "She's bald," he laughed. "Hairless as a bubble."

Katie laughed, too. "She is now, but a little time will take care of that."

"When will she keep her eyes open?"

"Soon, I'm sure. They've been open often, but only for a minute or two. She sleeps most of the time."

* * *

This new baby made life more interesting. And challenging. Of course, her arrival created changes and adjustments Katie and Kenny hadn't thought to prepare for.

Awakening in the middle of the night to a baby crying, headed the list. By the time Katie crawled out of bed and made it into the nursery, Kenny, too, awoke to the sound. He complained mightily about it. Moving the bassinet into their bedroom seemed to be the best solution. That way, the first cry from Marley would arouse Katie. She could get up, change the diaper, warm the baby's bottle and let Kenny sleep.

Within a few months Marley slept through the night. They returned her bassinet to the nursery. The three of them woke in the morning well rested.

Still reluctant to hold the baby, Kenny also refused to change a diaper or feed her a bottle.

"Kenny, just hold her on your lap for a few minutes. You'll get used to it."

"Nah, the kid's wiggly. And she pukes sometimes after a bottle."

"All part of being a baby. That's why I lift her over my shoulder and pat her back. To burp her. That helps. You should learn to do it."

"Ya do it fine. She don't need me smacking her on the back."

"Not *smack*, Kenny, *pat*. Gently. You just need to be careful."

"I don't wanna break her."

And so it went. Kenny would talk to Marley, even touch her, but couldn't bring himself to hold her. He seemed to be intimidated by how small she was. And so vulnerable. Or perhaps it was as simple as him not wanting to be involved in taking care of her, wanting no responsibility. Could he truly be that ambivalent about her? That lazy? Katie's concerns about what kind of a daddy he'd be were justified.

* * *

Little time passed before Katie realized total care for Marley fell on her shoulders. Although she loved Marley unconditionally, she expected Kenny to be a presence in the child's life. The way things were developing Katie would be in a position similar to a single parent.

These thoughts took Katie back to her own childhood. She'd lived in a home with both parents, but in reality a series of nannies raised her. She was never really close with her mother or her father. When she married Kenny, the gap between Katie and her parents widened. They made no effort to hide their disapproval of Kenny, and the disappointment they felt about the choice she'd made for a mate.

In spite of the family history, Katie let them know when she found out she was pregnant. After Marley was born she made a point to go see them every few months, when they weren't traveling . Aware of their intense dislike of Kenny she insisted that he not come along.

"So, I ain't good enough for yer uppity parents? They wanna see my kid, but don't have time fer me?"

"Well, Kenny, the three of you didn't get along well from the beginning. It was obvious you didn't like them and they weren't crazy about you. No effort was made, by either of you, to be on good terms. Things sort of got out of hand. So now that's just the way it is."

"Well, fuck 'em. I don't need 'em anyway. Just stay there a little while. I don't wanna hafta come looking for ya. It might get ugly."

And so it went. Only occasional visits, most often during Christmas season.

CHAPTER FORTY-ONE

Now, nearly two years old, toddling around and curious, Marley managed to get on Kenny's nerves. She'd grab his pack of cigarettes from the coffee table, empty it on the floor and play with them even put them in her mouth, always breaking several and generally making a mess. More than once she knocked over a beer he'd put on the floor beside his chair. Those things irritated him and he had trouble controlling his temper. With little provocation, he'd yell at her. "Dammit, Marley, keep ya paws off that."

He'd swat at her as though he was shooing away a nasty insect. That, in turn, infuriated Katie if she happened to catch him at it. Trying to explain the benefit of saying "no" to Marley in a normal tone of voice didn't help. Urging him to play with her, with her toys, simply made Kenny roll his eyes.

"How do ya play with a kid? Especially a girl kid?" he asked. "If it was a boy I could do something with cars, even toy cars. But a girl? With dolls or something fluffy? Not a chance."

Recently, hearing Marley scream and cry, sent Katie rushing into the living room. Kenny held Marley by one arm, lifting and shaking her as she tried to squirm away from him. Katie pulled the little girl away before he could do worse. Raising her own voice to Kenny, she said, "You do *not* lift a child by the arm! Are you nuts?"

"Well, the brat spit her milk at me. Ya gonna say that's okay?"

"No, it isn't okay at all. But you need to *teach* her. She wasn't born knowing what you want or how to behave. Besides, you just don't treat a kid, well, *anyone,* like that. You might have yanked her arm right out of its socket. You hurt her and she probably has no idea why you did it."

"I'm tryin' to teach her a lesson."

"Think about it. That's not the way to do it. There are better ways. Ways that aren't so rough. Have some patience. She's still a baby."

"Well, ya better keep her outta my way. And make her leave my stuff alone."

"Kenny, put your *stuff* away. Keep it out of her reach. She doesn't need anything of yours to play with. She has toys."

"She'd better start learning what ain't hers, and play with her own toys, not mine."

"Honest to god, Kenny, you sound like a child yourself. You're old enough to know better. And, if you keep yelling at her and yanking her around like she's a dishrag, she's going to be afraid of you. Maybe worse, she might learn to hate you."

"Nah, she won't hate me. I'm her daddy."

"Stranger things have happened."

* * *

Katie loved Marley more than she'd imagined she could love anyone. It could be consuming. She would protect the child with her own life. *Something about being a mother has changed my habits. My thoughts, plans for the future. I need to remember to keep all those things in perspective. I must be careful not to evolve into someone who emotionally smothers her child.*

Marley is healthy and smart and cute. With a solid home life and a good education she'll likely develop into a well-rounded young woman. That's all I want for her. I need to work on getting

Kenny calmed down. He's supposed to be part of this, too.

It seemed to her that Kenny had lost the awe he'd first felt for Marley and now found her more a nuisance than anything else.

Katie's love for Kenny had been a different kind, and though she didn't want to admit it, or think about it, that love had weakened considerably during the past two or three years.

* * *

Marley would be four in April. Their neighborhood had no children close to her age, thus leaving her without playmates. For such a young child, life could be boring with no one to play with. Development of social skills would suffer, possibly causing problems as she grew older. Katie considered enrolling her in a pre-school program and returning to work herself. Starting Pre-Kindergarten in September would be perfect. Katie could go back to teaching at the same time.

She contacted a couple of the teachers she'd worked with. They'd been in the school system much longer than Katie had. She sought their advice. They gave her the information she wanted about a good Pre-K program. It took less than a month to make a decision and arrangements for what she thought would be the best for Marley. Getting back to work would be good for her, and Marley would have a solid start for kindergarten after she turned five.

CHAPTER FORTY-TWO

The phone rang. Katie answered it.

"Hello, mother, how are you? And how's father?"

"Your father and I are both doing quite well, Katie. Thank you."

"Are you enjoying retirement?"

"We are, indeed."

"Do you have plans for more traveling?"

"As a matter of fact, that's the purpose of my call."

"Oh? Where are you going this time?" She bit her tongue. *That sounded a little sarcastic, or bitter or something. Don't want her mad at me.*

"We've booked a fabulous cruise. We'll make stops at dozens of places across Europe. This will be for pleasure, not business. A nice change. We'll be away quite a long time. Maybe as much as two years."

"That *is* a long time. I can't remember you ever being away from home that long."

"We haven't. This will be a new experience. We'll close the house for the duration."

"I do hope you have a wonderful time. It sounds exciting."

A lull in the conversation, then, "Katie, the holidays are approaching. You will bring Marley to visit won't you? We're leaving in early January."

"Yes, mother, of course I will."

"I'd like it if you'd come to the house twice this year, instead of only once. Do you think you will be able to do that?"

"I'm sure I can. I'll make it a point to."

"And, Katie, as always, please have it just the two of you. Don't allow Kenny to tag along."

"I know, mother. He won't be with us."

After they checked schedules and selected two dates that satisfied them both, the conversation was over.

* * *

Katie fell into a moment of reverie: she brought Marley to visit her parents each Christmas season. They'd been wonderful to her every time, almost as though they regretted not treating Katie better when she was a youngster. As though they were trying to make up for her childhood, and maybe the rest of the year, as well, when they ignored both Marley and Katie. A strange situation. It seemed they thoroughly enjoyed being grandparents.

It wasn't simply that they gave lovely, appropriate, expensive gifts, which they did, but there was true love exhibited. Hugs, kisses and loving words, that seemed genuine, were shared between Marley and both grandparents. There were times Katie considered not going to her parent's home no matter the occasion. It didn't seem right to get together so few days each year. But she went anyway. It seemed worse for Marley to grow up never seeing her grandparents or knowing anything about them.

They cherished Marley. She'd brought a new perspective into their lives and added joy. Katie secretly hoped her parent's love for Marley would overflow, landing on her as well.

She was truly baffled as to why visits with Katie and Marley, once or twice a year was enough for them. Thinking about the future jolted her brain. Suppose sometime she really needed help? Someone to depend on? Could she count on her folks for anything? She wanted to ask them to explain, but chose not to, afraid they'd decide to cut ties altogether.

The Millfords believed she'd made an abysmal choice for a husband. They both despised Kenny. Neither could explain why, nor did they try. But to have him permanently out of their daughter's life, and more so their grandchild's life, would satisfy them. Whatever method used to accomplish that mattered not a whit. Once, but only once, her father had mentioned a thirty-eight revolver hidden away in his closet. Just in case Katie should ever need it. She knew how to find it.

* * *

When the subject of divorce between Katie and Kenny became an issue, the Millfords were out of the country and hadn't any idea of what the future might hold in store for their only child and grandchild. Even if they had known, they would have been powerless to do anything about it. Possibly would not have considered trying to do anything at all. The choice to ignore family difficulties, as they'd always been so adept at doing, was made.

During their travels abroad they were unaware that at home, Kenny harbored serious plans for revenge he felt due Katie. Only he could comprehend the reasons.

CHAPTER FORTY-THREE

By prior arrangement, one Friday Susan picked up Marley from school. She'd take her to watch a kids' movie, then keep Marley with her for the weekend. Susan had become Aunt Susan. They both loved every minute of it.

When Kenny came home from work Katie stood by the kitchen counter completing the final touches the night's dinner. An old Beatles song played on the radio. Kenny opened the fridge, grabbed a Bud and sat down at the table.

"Turn off that goddam hippie music." he ordered.

"If you don't like it, that's tough," replied Katie. "I do."

"Woman," said Kenny. "I reckon ya didn't hear me right. I want that long-haired hippie shit *off*. Either yer gonna do it or I will."

Turning around, Katie studied him to gauge his anger on a scale of one to ten. Deciding it no higher than a three she said, "You want it off? Turn it off."

Her assessment proved correct. He was just trying to pull a power play. Nevertheless, he reached up to the shelf that held several cookbooks and the radio. He flicked the switch to off.

After taking a gulp of beer he asked, "How soon's dinner?"

"Only a few minutes," Katie told him as she arranged the dishes and silverware at their places on the table.

"What ya fixin'?"

"Chicken Divan. I saw the recipe in a magazine a few months ago. Looks real good." Katie showed him the color picture of chicken, broccoli and noodles in a creamy sauce.

"Well, ya know, Kates, I'll just take a bologna sandwich. That stuff don't look all that great to me."

"I've already prepared one dinner. You want a sandwich? Fix it yourself."

He slapped a couple of slices of bologna between two heavily-mayonnaised pieces of bread, grabbed a handful of chips and another beer and went into the living room to watch the evening news and sports reports on television.

Keep it up. Pretty soon you can eat bologna sandwiches three meals a day if you want to!

They avoided each other the rest of the night. By morning old grudges were remembered and new grudges began to build.

CHAPTER FORTY-FOUR

Being a Saturday, and off work, Kenny called Elwood and asked him to come by to help steam-clean the engine in his car. In reality, he wanted Elwood there so he could vent to him about Katie. Kenny's mood was dark. Bitterness burned in his belly.

He stood in the garage trying to concentrate on what he wanted to do. He lifted the hood and studied the engine. Keeping his mind straight, and working out a plan for the project, seemed impossible. Focus just wasn't there. Animosity from the night before had spilled over into this morning he and Katie had continued arguing half the day. He finally quit yelling and headed into the garage. By the time Elwood got there Kenny's fury raged like a forest fire.

* * *

Katie remained exasperated, too. But keeping with her own routine she began to straighten up the kitchen. The garage door stood open. She couldn't help but overhear part of the conversation going on between the two men.

"I ought to fuckin' kill her," Kenny said. "Maybe both of 'em."

"Aw, man, you can't do that," said Elwood. "That's your wife and kid, there. You're talking crazy."

" Remember Lizzie? I *could* do it. Lizzie was just Lizzie. There wasn't no baby involved there. But this one spends more time with the kid than she does with me. And bitch, bitch, bitch about my smokes. About my beer. A guy has to have something of his own, don't he? Don't I bring in a paycheck every week? She needs to stay off my case."

"You're just mad now, and Lizzie's ancient history. You'd

be smart to forget about that one. Lucky you didn't get nailed," Elwood reminded him. "Chill out. Things have changed since Marley came along. Give it time."

"Shit, Elwood, ya sound bad as she does. Marley's not a baby any more. How long do I gotta to wait for things to get back to normal?"

"A kid changes your life forever. There is no more normal. But yeah, women are rough to handle. Moody, and all. But, you know, she works, too. She dumps some bucks into the kitty. I reckon you weren't cut out to be a daddy. You can't change all that now."

"Well, I'm gonna buy a good shovel. I could bury both of 'em here by the garage. Plant a little bed of flowers right over top 'em. She likes flowers. Ya can buy some already growing in pots. Just dig a hole and dump 'em in the ground. They'd grow up nice and pretty."

"Kenny, shut up. That's scary talk. Stupid talk. And you know it. You're just mad at her again. Calm down and forget about this shit. Time to grow up. She's good to you." An awkward pause. Then, trying to change the subject: "You want a beer?"

"Ya got something going on about her? Yer on her side all the time. Keep runnin' yer mouth and ya'll end up in the hole right along side 'em."

* * *

Those words made Katie's legs go weak. Barely able to stand, she held onto the kitchen sink to keep from collapsing to the floor. The shocking picture that emerged in her mind made her tremble: Kenny, holding a shovel in his hand, standing over

153

Marley's dead body. *I swear if I had a gun I'd shoot him between the eyes this minute. Point blank range. Just for even thinking that.*

* * *

Elwood made an appropriate exit, leaving them alone for dinner. Through the meal both remained mute, whipped into a froth of quiet rage. Most of whatever they'd argued about seemed forgotten now, replaced with newer, bizarre mental visions. Even Marley sensed something terribly wrong floated in the air. She kept unusually quiet.

Once everything in the kitchen looked neat and tidy again, Katie felt her stomach begin to roil. Her nervousness took over. She headed to the bathroom and vomited until she felt she'd pass out.

After work Monday, Katie hurried home anxious to be sure to get there before Kenny. Playing a hunch she went straight to the garage. A shiny new shovel sat propped in a corner against the back wall.

Holy shit! I'm not ready to die

CHAPTER FORTY-FIVE

The next day she left work early. She drove to a police station close to home, intending to file a complaint of some sort.

Believing a policeman could advise her, she detailed the recent conversation to an officer.

"Mrs. Hagen," he replied. "There's nothing we can do about it. We are not in the business of settling domestic differences. And you're telling me this is something you *overheard*? He's not even threatened you."

"You think the new shovel means nothing? That it's not a threat? After what he said? What am I supposed to do?"

"Talk it over with him. He probably stayed angry after the two of you argued. How many times have you heard someone say 'I could just kill you'? Happens every day. Rare that anyone actually acts on it. Consequences are steep."

"Well, I'm terrified. I don't believe I can trust him. And, I can tell that Marley, our little girl, feels uneasy, too. Does a father ever kill his own kid?"

"We've heard of a few. Usually it's the mother who does that, though. I've never been involved in either type of case. And I don't want to be. It gets ugly."

* * *

"Kenny," Katie started, "I was putting a few things in the garage the other day."

"Yeah, so?"

"Well, I saw a shovel back in the corner. I don't remember it being there before. Looks new. What's it for?" A terrible rumbling ignited through her body. She felt it reach out and grab every nerve. Her hands shook. She stuffed them into her pockets to keep them out of sight. She didn't want to give him a clue how terrified she felt. She knew he'd feed off that. Use it to his benefit. Sweat from her armpits crawled down both sides of her ribcage. She hoped it didn't leave tell-tale wet patches on her shirt.

She saw his face harden. "Uh, ah, Kates…it's for *ya*."

"For me? Really? How so?" *My voice feels so shaky. Does it sound that way to him, or only to me, in my head?*

"Yeah, well I saw ya digging in the yard with some little tiny tool so ya could plant some flowers. Thought a sturdy shovel might make yer job a little easier."

Katie watched his mouth form a smile. She sucked in a deep breath noticing that his eyes refused to follow suit. They glowed like a demon's.

She didn't buy anything he'd said. Certainly he'd guess that she'd be on her toes now.

She wondered if he thought she'd overheard some of that conversation he'd had with Elwood.

* * *

He wondered if Elwood had mentioned something about it to Katie.

CHAPTER FORTY-SIX

This called for serious action. Fast action. Pulling information from all available resources Katie decided to quit teaching and go for the gold. If, no, *when*, she and Kenny split up she would need a better income. Her seven-year-old car might have one good year left in it. The mileage steadily crept higher. Soon she'd need a replacement. With only her salary to depend on, money would become an issue.

Marley would be five in a week. School would be out two months after that. A suitable escape might be worked out by then. She'd have to keep quiet about it and let nothing slip out to foil her plans. That would be tricky. Extra vigilance must be used now. Keeping a step or two ahead and having a watchful eye at all times might save them from a life or death situation.

Finding an abundance of office positions advertised in the newspaper, she began filling out applications and carefully scheduling interviews during the next few weeks. After a dozen or more, with three solid offers, one company gave a tempting proposition. In addition to a sizable increase to her current salary, as well as good benefits, this business had eleven offices scattered throughout the United States. That could be an ace in the hole. If she went to work there, after a while she might be able to remain with the same firm but move hundreds of miles away. Then she and Marley could feel safe. She accepted the position. She was scheduled to begin one month after the close of school for summer break.

She enrolled Marley in a year-round private school only two blocks from the location of her new job. Couldn't be more convenient. During the process, information about the difficulties existing with Kenny was brought out in the open. The school guaranteed they would protect her privacy. No one would be given any information unless Katie had authorized it advance, in writing. A huge load slipped off her shoulders. Worries that Kenny might try to take Marley from school, or worse, do something to hurt her, filled Katie's mind to the point of distraction every day. Relief blossomed with this cooperation,

CHAPTER FORTY-SEVEN

When they were first married, Katie determined divorce would never be an option. She vowed their names would not be added to the statistics. *Of course arguments will happen. Difficulties will arise. We will not agree on everything. We'll work it out.* She knew no union was perfect.

With every major challenge faced, she'd rise and fight again. For a long time she remained relentless, struggling to save their marriage. *There must be a way to solve this.*

After teetering on a delicate balance for years, divorce not only seemed to be the best solution, there was no other true choice. Something she never considered in the beginning, or even the middle, had been added: physical harm. Danger had been thrown into the equation. Danger not only for herself, but worse, for Marley. The time had come to walk away. Now.

Kenny's threats had not been repeated. Those words haunted her. They stayed in the back of her mind urging her to move on. Waiting around for another, possibly worse, act of retaliation from Kenny, she could not ride it through. She and Marley would get out of there, soon. Away from him and be safe. And have a normal life.

* * *

When Katie told Kenny she could no longer go on living with him he was shocked.

Then angry. He didn't believe she meant it.

"Fine, if ya want a divorce I'll give ya one. Should I wrap it, and tie a bow around it? And, by the way, would that be for birthday or for Christmas?" Storming into another room, he pushed the door making sure it would bang on his way out.

A few days later she said, "Kenny, I'm not kidding. We need to get a divorce."

He growled at her. "Yer serious ain't ya?" he asked. "Well, listen up. I ain't givin' ya no divorce. If we ever get a divorce it'll be because *I* decide to get one. Can ya fit *that* into yer head?"

"You're wrong this time, buddy." The divorce proceedings were about to begin.

* * *

Following the recommendation of Susan's husband, Joe, Katie contacted a divorce attorney who agreed to handle the case for her. She told him it might be ugly, and it certainly would not be easy, but it was very necessary. After several visits to his office during a couple of weeks, the divorce papers were completed. Katie brought a copy home and presented them to Kenny to read and sign. Handing them to him, she explained what they were. She knew he'd fly into a crazed rage. He did.

"Goddamit, Katie, I already tol' ya. No freakin' divorce. Ya married me, bitch, and ya'll stay married to me. Ya snotty little shit, what the hell is wrong with ya?" He tossed the papers toward the ceiling, both arms dancing in the air. Glaring at Katie, still waving his arms wildly he said, "How many times do I have to tell ya that, for chrissake? This ain't happenin'. Take them papers and stuff 'em up yer lawyer's ass!"

Through sheer determination, over time she'd fine-tuned her own technique to keep calm, with anger in check, when he went over the edge like this. Her resolve kicked into high gear now.

"Kenny, you may or may not like it. You may or may not

fight it. But it *is* going to happen. And soon. You can throw the papers to the ceiling all day and all night. Who cares? There are more."

Creature of habit, she turned back to the refrigerator to get things out to start dinner. Over her shoulder she said, "Oh, by the way, I think you ought to get yourself a lawyer. I won't be discussing this with you anymore. And stop your yelling and cussing. You'll get Marley to start crying again."

He snatched the Zippo and a pack of cigarettes off the kitchen counter and stuffed them into his shirt pocket. Grabbing his keys from an end table by the sofa, he burst out of the house, slamming the door behind him.

Several hours after midnight he returned, stinking of beer and cigarette smoke. He crawled into bed beside her. Snuggling close, he slid his rough hand under her nightgown and up between her legs. She knew he hoped to arouse her. Repulsed, she pushed him away, and hissed, "Leave me be. You smell like a pig."

Getting out of bed she headed for the spare room. Elwood was already sleeping there, snoring loudly, a disgusting odor wafting off his body. Taking a cover from the closet, she spent the remainder of the night on the floor in Marley's room.

CHAPTER FORTY-EIGHT

With the divorce in the works Katie put a deposit on an apartment a few miles from their house. No one asked questions when she used her maiden name on the rental application. It would be available for her to move into in a month. Calling C & P Telephone Company and arranging for an unlisted phone number seemed like a huge step to take, but it went through without a hitch. If she had to have contact with Kenny it would be in public on neutral ground. Safety for herself and Marley took priority over everything else. They needed to get out of the house. As soon as possible.

After she rented a storage unit to hold belongings temporarily, little by little she loaded the car with her belongings, and Marley's. While Kenny was at work and Marley in school, it didn't take long to get the job done. Whatever she left behind he could do with as he pleased.

* * *

Throughout the ordeal Susan stood by Katie, always offering a shoulder to cry on, an ear to listen. Knowing Katie was serious, and would not back down, Susan feared for the safety of her best friend if she didn't get away from Kenny soon. He seemed bent on destruction.

"You know, I tried to tell you long ago that I felt he'd hurt you. But you were in love and didn't want to hear it. Now, Katie, I'd like for you to come and stay with Joe and me. Bring Marley with you. Right away. You'll both stay here until permanent arrangements are made."

"Susan, I appreciate it, but you know your place is the first one Kenny will look for me."

"I know that. But I have the problem solved. At least for a little while."

"How?"

"Well, the neighbors behind us have a garage that opens into the back alley between our houses. They're leaving next week to go on a month-long cruise to the islands. I've arranged for you to park your car there while they're gone. I have the garage door key. It will be perfect. Kenny can drive by here all he wants. He won't see your car anywhere in the neighborhood."

"God, Susan, you certainly have gone above and beyond the call. And Joe won't mind? The two of us, one a five-year-old, crashing here for a week?"

"Katie, Joe knows we're like sisters. He not only doesn't mind, he suggested it. He loves you both, too, and knows what an idiot Kenny has been for a long time. We have a big house, and it's just Joe and me. There's plenty of room. We think you should stay here the whole month our neighbors are away."

"I don't know. A month. That's a long time. I don't want to be responsible for ruining our friendship."

"Dammit, Katie, listen to you! There's a lot on the line. We all get along, and thirty days is nothing in the grand scheme of things. Don't think about it any more. Just come here and stay. Slide into comfort. And safety."

Wheels in Katie's head spun while she thought about it. In a moment she decided. "I'll do it. But you will have to swear and promise that I can handle my share of the work, cooking and cleaning and all that. And I'll chip in some money as well. It won't be much at first. But I start the new job soon. I should be able to help."

"Yeah, you can help with the work around here for sure. I won't let you think you're a princess, or on vacation. You're family. Get used to it." Susan laughed.

"Well, I'll need to be especially careful and change my regular routine. I'll drive Marley to school, then I'll go to work. I can't move into the apartment for a month anyway. So your plan seems flawless."

"Perfect. Then you'll be here when? Monday?"

"Yes. I will. It's the best thing to do, I think. The safest. You realize you may be saving my life?"

CHAPTER FORTY-NINE

On Katie's last day at the Silver Spring house, her home for several years, Susan agreed to pick up Marley from school, taking her home with her. Katie would be there later, after a double-check to be sure nothing remained that she need take with her. All household goods and furniture now belonged to Kenny to use or get rid of. She'd say a final goodbye to Kenny, hoping to make a civil exit.

Waiting in the living room for him to come home from work pitched her into a hollowness of emotion. Complete emptiness. This would be difficult. She felt flat, like a stick figure, but she came mentally prepared. She'd told him she'd be there. For the last time. Although desperate to leave, to get out, get away from him and not feel threatened, she kept sitting there, clinging to the thought that this behavior was the right thing to do. Leaving on good terms should settle the dust of failure and sadness.

But, desperation often forces a decision that may not result in a positive outcome.

* * *

By nine o'clock, the time to leave had come and gone. Katie felt angry and bored. The wait had been much too long already. *What a fool I've been to believe this would matter. I won't devote another moment of this night to him.* She picked up her purse, slung it over her shoulder and headed to the door. Wrapping her fingers around the knob she felt it turn. From the outside.

It flew open nearly knocking her to the floor. Kenny burst in, staggering. He was hammered.

Throwing his arm around her shoulders he pulled her to the

sofa and shoved her down. She tried to stand. He pushed her back onto the soft cushions.

"Ya ain't goin' nowhere," he said.

"Kenny, I…"

"Shut up. Ya'll go when I tell ya." He dragged a chair across the floor, positioned it directly across from where she sat, and flopped into it. He sat with one leg bent at the knee, its ankle resting across the opposite knee.

She stared at him. With a shock she realized, for the first time, he'd carried in a rifle. It now lay across his folded leg. His hand rested on the stock.

"So, Kates, whatcha gotta say? Watcha gonna do now?"

"Kenny, you know I just came here to say goodbye. There is nothing left to say. We've said it all. We've said too much."

"Nah, I don' think so."

Katie stood. "Yes, it's all been said. Over and over. I waited here tonight just hoping to have a peaceful ending. Apparently you have other ideas."

He lumbered up from the chair and reeled towards her, moving with slow, deliberate, clumsy steps.

"Yup, reckon I do at that. Ya'll sit right back down there now, ya hear?" With one hand he pushed her onto the sofa once more.

Shouldering the rifle he left the room, waddling side to side like a duck. When he was out of sight Katie stood again, quietly sneaking her way to the door. As she reached for the door knob the sound of his hand slapping on the wood stock of the rifle froze her to the spot. She heard him hoist it into position. She dropped to her knees as the click of the trigger sent a bullet smashing into the wall a few feet from where she had just stood. The noise was deafening. She thought she felt the room shake.

"I *tol'* ya ta stay right there!"

Still crouching, she watched him shuffle back to the kitchen, then return with a six-pack of Bud. Placing the beer on the floor near his chair, he pointed the rifle at her. "Now, Kates-baby, get your ass back over there and sit a while. I ain't done wit' ya."

Not saying a word, she rose, followed his orders, and returned to the sofa. Her mind whirled, searching to form a plan to get the hell out of there.

"Now, Kates, tell me again, whatcha gonna do?"

Refusing to answer, she watched as he popped a top and took a long, deep swig.

"Nuttin' to say, huh?" Another gulp. Then another.

She remained silent.

Another swallow. Empty now. Pop another top. Chug, chug.

"Ya, know, Kates, I can sit here all night, waitin' for an answer." Swig. Another empty. Let it fall to the floor, opened the next one. Kept it up til all were gone. "I got nuttin' to do."

She watched his face as his eyes glazed over. They looked more like glass eyes than real ones, or toys to go with a Halloween costume. She could tell they didn't register the scene around him. Their lids crept down blocking reality from his view.

The thought of the six beers he'd just consumed, in addition to who knew how many more before he came home, made Katie stare at him, transfixed. Kenny, in his drunken haze, leaned toward her. His fingers relaxed and he lost his grip on the rifle. It clattered noisily to the floor.

Kenny didn't flinch.

His eyes stayed closed, his mouth hung slack and open.

As she watched in utter awe he slid off the chair, landing in a lumpy pile on the floor beside the weapon.

"Kenny?" she called, barely above a whisper.

No answer.

A little louder, "Kenny?"

It appeared he didn't hear her. *Is he really out? Or is he setting a trap?*

CHAPTER FIFTY

Katie approached with caution and nudged him with the toe of her shoe. Nothing. A little harder. Still no response. Bending down she lifted the rifle. It was heavier than she'd thought it would be. Raising it to her shoulder she aimed at him. Realizing she hadn't the faintest idea of how to shoot it gave her only regret, not a tinge of guilt.

After slipping her shoes off, she slung her handbag over one shoulder and the rifle over the other. Carrying the shoes, tip-toeing to the front door, and out, she took great care not to let it slam.

Letting the rifle disappear into the hedges in front of the house, bolting to her car consumed her thoughts.

The mental vision of how the marriage had unraveled so thoroughly haunted her. It seemed that over the years he'd reached the point that Kenny felt no guilt or sense of conscience. And that he trusted no one, hiding dark thoughts behind that lopsided grin he offered on the outside. She'd learned that although he was quick to anger, he remained adept at hiding other emotions. Even more devious than she'd had any idea about. Katie believed viciousness blended into his blood. It could never be washed away.

No turning back now. She felt desperate to get off the crazy merry-go-round.

A sudden burst of energy propelled her forward. Her anger was sucked to the surface like venom from a snake bite. *I should have shot the bastard*

* * *

Efforts to slip the key into the ignition were unsuccessful. Her hand shook violently. It took several attempts before she managed to connect and get the car started. Once that was accomplished more trembling throughout her body prevented her from driving. Then, fearful of discovery but weak with relief, the success of the escape came into clear focus. The illusion of safety intoxicated her. Shifting the car into gear she sped away.

Katie thought about Marley staying with Susan, and knew Susan would keep her safe. Adrenalin fueled the feeling of a new freedom. She guided the car out onto the main thoroughfare, then, instead of going straight home, raced toward the country.

Without city street-lights the blacktop seemed to disappear into eternal darkness. Within a few miles, the only glow came from the headlights of her vehicle. On she drove, her car hungrily swallowing up the white dotted line dividing the road into lanes.

The line became a fixation. Hypnotic. With no traffic, and utter darkness all around, there was nothing else to look at. She felt tired. Getting drowsy, she clicked on the radio, jiggling the dial hoping to find some music to help keep her awake. Maybe something to sing along with.

An unfamiliar station came on. The reception was poor. She thought she heard an announcer say something about Cincinnati, Ohio. Miles and miles away. Audio levels kept changing, music bounced in and out. For a while it provided some company, but not much. Rolling down the window, the cool breeze felt good against her face. Soon the night air turned chilly. She rolled it back up.

Mile after monotonous mile she pushed on. The radio faded completely. She took no notice. Her eyelids fluttered. Then closed. She nodded off. The car slowed and drifted onto the narrow gravel shoulder. Katie's hands hung loose on the wheel.

Rough terrain beneath the tires jolted her awake. As her head pulled up with a start, her fingers tightened around the wheel. The beam of her own headlights aimed down the side of a hill ending in inky darkness. It threw her into a panic. Without being aware of why, she jerked the steering wheel to the left. The car leapt back onto the road and skidded sideways. Slamming on the brake, the car continued to slide over the crunchy gravel and turned a little more, but she managed to bring it to a stop.

Moving her foot from the brake pedal to the accelerator, slowly she righted the vehicle. A quiver convulsed her body. Her legs shook so badly she couldn't keep even pressure on the pedal to supply fuel to the engine. Once she realized she'd fallen asleep her mind felt like it might explode. If, in her terror, she had pulled the wheel to the right instead of the left she'd have soared down the embankment. Possibly gotten seriously hurt. Maybe even killed. *Sweet Jesus! That was a close call. I didn't know I was that tired. It certainly woke me up.*

She drove slowly, moving forward with extra care, giving her nerves a chance to settle down. Although her heart still pounded, the shaking subsided. Half an hour passed before true comfort set in. Little by little the needle on the speedometer crept up to the fifty-five mile an hour speed limit. At last, turning around to go home, she motored on. Normal breathing returned. *I'm all right now.*

The dashboard clock read three-thirty. Early morning. Hours had passed since Katie had seen anything but dark sky and blackness all around her. Now an occasional truck rumbled by going in the opposite direction. *Returning from a produce delivery to a market? At least I might be entering civilization again.*

Her journey continued homeward.

CHAPTER FIFTY-ONE

The sound of the horn blared so loud and so close that it seemed to be coming from inside her body. Katie snapped to attention. Staring into the high beams of an eighteen-wheeler momentarily paralyzed her with fear. Gripping the steering wheel, she veered back into her own lane. The truck driver swerved the other way onto the shoulder to his right, desperately trying to avoid a head-on collision. As he edged past, they were so close that the two of them could have reached out their windows and shook hands.

This time, sufficient fright took hold. She'd nearly wet her pants. After coming close to running down the side of the hill just a little while ago she'd felt awake and alert. In control and quite capable of driving on.

She was wrong. And this near miss could have cost her life.

The shakes took over again. Now, deliberately pulling off the road onto the shoulder, she turned the key shutting off the engine. Near hysteria, her thoughts jumbled, refusing to get in order. She must relax. *Calm down, kiddo. Get your act together. Drive just til you can find a safe place to park and catch an hour of sleep.*

Feeling as though she'd been functioning as if in a trance, she started the car up again. The sky showed signs that dawn would be breaking in another hour. Dim light revealed the shapes of a few houses set far back off the road. And trees came into view. *Lots* of trees.

Ah, a road sign. But the sign was bent over at the top, the words weren't visible. How far had she driven? She'd been on the road more than five hours. Two-hundred miles? More? The gas gauge hovered near the empty marker.

Soon another sign: Welcome to Maryland. Exiting the roadway into the first full-service rest stop, she made her way to the back of the area, parked and locked the doors. Curling up on the front seat she slept.

A knock on the window aroused her. A man in a uniform stood there: a cop. Rolling down the window, she offered a weak smile. "Hi, I nearly fell asleep while driving home. Didn't want to have an accident so I pulled in here to catch a nap."

"Well, time to move on. This isn't the Ritz Carlton. A woman alone shouldn't be trying to sleep here. Bad things can happen."

"Okay, I know you're right. I'll gas up and get going. Do you know how far it is to Silver Spring?"

"About forty miles. Sun's coming up so rush hour is starting. You'd better get a move on or it'll take longer to get there than you want it to."

"Thanks, I'm on my way."

The cop, wanting to be sure she left, watched as Katie's car was fueled up and the windows cleaned off.

Katie headed south, grateful Marley had spent the night with Susan.

Once home, the events of the night flooded her with renewed fear. She slept a few hours. Later in the morning, repeating the events aloud to Susan forced the memory, making it seem that she was right in front of Kenny again. A sobering moment.

* * *

While they stayed the month with Susan and Joe, Katie used their neighbor's garage as a hiding place for her car. The neighbors returned from island-hopping, happy, yet exhausted. They decided they needed a change of pace at home. With each of them nearing seventy, they felt their house was too big, and more work than they wanted to deal with at this stage of their lives. Plans to move into a retirement community seemed not only logical, but exciting. That meant putting the house on the market, and making arrangements to sell it.

The timing couldn't have been better. Katie struggled to work out financing to buy it. If successful, it meant a huge relief for all concerned. For the first time in a long while Katie had the odds fall to her side. She canceled the lease on the apartment and moved their meager belongings from the storage unit into the house behind Susan and Joe's. A perfect solution.

CHAPTER FIFTY-TWO

During the months after Katie filed for divorce, Kenny often phoned her at work pleading for her to reconsider and take him back. Wild promises were made: he'd quit drinking; give up smoking; stop the cussing and swearing. Even more important, there would be no more physical threats. He'd keep them under tight control. If she still wanted to go for counseling he'd do that, too. Whatever it took. He loved her; had always loved her; and needed her. He would pay proper attention to Marley and not treat her like a nuisance, or leave her alone like a book on a shelf.

Numb to anything Kenny had to offer, Katie always responded with an absolute no. There was no persuading her. Whatever she had felt for him in the past he'd killed in a hundred ways. Still, sadness that the marriage had come to this swept over her. The two of them had never been a good match. From the beginning she'd been giddy and used very poor judgment.

The divorce was final January twenty-eighth. Although a few days past her birthday, it was the best present in years. *Is it finally over?*

CHAPTER FIFTY-THREE

As usual, Katie called to let Susan know she was on the way home. She'd changed her route from work and made arrangements for Marley to have special transportation from school to Susan's. She must keep her child out of harm's way. Too many weird things kept happening. Some, she felt sure, had been designed by Kenny. There were others she thought might be attributed to him, but might be simple coincidence. Wondering if she was being paranoid she refused to allow herself to worry about absolutely everything.

Keeping an eye out for the unusual, she went along her way, driving yet another convoluted pattern. She had mapped out several routes, some taking her to work and others returning to the neighborhood where both she and Susan lived. Driving along some of these back roads seemed like a good idea at the time, they had little traffic. But that was disconcerting, and gave her the feeling of being the proverbial sitting duck. *Tomorrow I will figure a better way even if I'm forced to be out in the crunch of rush hour. It might take me a little longer to get home, but I'll feel safer.*

* * *

She heard his car before she saw it. Wheels squealed as he rounded the corner coming after her.

Katie knew the timing would be exactly as he wanted. No car in his sight now but hers. His control at the wheel proved spectacular as always. He slowed down to assess the area as he neared, and then accelerated.

Terrified, she sped up and tried to outrun him. Soon, she admitted to herself there was no way in the world she could. Instead, she pulled her vehicle to the side of the empty street bumping up onto the curb, out of his path.

He adjusted position and drove directly at her.

Knowing there was not enough time to get out of the car to safety, and feeling close to death, she bent over onto the passenger seat burying her head under her hands and arms for protection.

The sound of roaring engine and screaming tires closing in stole her breath. "You sonofabitch!" She gasped. Her heart wrestled in her chest as though trying to break free and make a run for safety. Holding her body rigid till every muscle ached seemed to be the only thing time allowed her to do.

Hearing the swoosh of his vehicle as it passed within inches forced a scream to explode from her lips.

He cut back with graceful precision leaving no mark on either car, yet making her smaller vehicle tremble. Continuing up the street, he gave one short toot on his horn as a further insult. In an instant he slowed down to the speed limit.

She knew he did not look back.

This was the third time in the last several weeks he had openly threatened her in one way or another. Being truly frightened of him, she knew his twisted mind held a wealth of punishments. Any of them had the power to terrify her yet keep him from being identified as the perpetrator. That 'he said/she said' thing.

CHAPTER FIFTY-FOUR

A month crept by and nothing happened to hold her poised on the edge of terror. Still, she continued to leave work by the rear exit that only employees and delivery people knew of. Unable to quiet her nerves and feel life had returned to normal, her stomach felt upset much of the time. She skipped meals and lost weight. Difficulty concentrating on her workload presented even more problems. She couldn't allow this to put her job in jeopardy. Serious thought about applying for a transfer hovered constantly in her mind. The satellite office in Virginia could be an option. If that worked out she'd take Marley and move. That might not solve the entire problem, but at least she would not be a target within such easy reach.

A little checking produced the information that in a few months a woman in the Virginia office would be taking maternity leave. Rumor had it she'd not return to work, and the position would be open. If Katie applied for, and was accepted to the job, it would be a slight step down, but there would be opportunities to move back up the ladder quickly. No hurry, she had time to think about it. She'd need to rent out the house behind Susan's they'd grown to enjoy so much. That thought saddened her. But, right now, getting away from this area seemed something to give thorough attention to. Not only for herself, but for Marley. The little girl's whole life was ahead of her. That must not be grabbed from her because of a crazed man.

Another two weeks passed without further incident. Relaxing a little, she held dim hope this horror might be over.

Although different from teaching a classroom full of young students, she enjoyed her work. Tasks were going well, her job there moved along smoothly.

The new receptionist put a call through to her.

She answered. "Hello, this is Katie."

"Hi, Kates," glued her to her chair. She held the receiver a moment too long.

Not moving quickly enough to return the receiver to the cradle, and disconnect the call, she heard Kenny yell, "Hey, Kates, now don't hang up on me. I'm calling to give ya good news." He sounded happy, cheerful for the first time in ages. Maybe years.

Automatically she put the phone back to her ear. "What?" It was difficult to get even one word out.

"Well, Kates, I know I've put ya through some rough times here lately. I jus' want ya to know that's all over. I was a dumbass. I know ya ain't comin' back so I found me someone else! No need to be worried no more."

"Why...why, Kenny," she stuttered. "That's wonderful! I appreciate the call and I sincerely wish both of you the best. Thanks for letting me know." Her throat constricted. Her stomach fought to keep her lunch from escaping and spewing all over her desk. Could he be telling the truth?

CHAPTER FIFTY-FIVE

For the next several weeks Katie realized she was watching her rear view mirror almost as much as she watched the vehicles cutting in and out of traffic in front of her. The alternate routes home proved to be successful. The strain of living in forced seclusion began to relax.

Ownership of the house behind Susan's continued to be ideal. Happily, Katie only needed to change her footwear from high heels to tennis shoes for the quiet walk across the heavily treed yards to Susan's back door. Little by little a comfort level settled in. She didn't jump at every unusual noise any more. She could smile at strangers again. Relief spread from her to Susan. Gradually the two of them dared to go shopping together or to a movie or out to dinner somewhere. Joe, bless his heart, offered to take care of Marley while they were gone.

Still leery, and not trusting Kenny, they never took Katie's car. The method of concealing it had worked for months. Katie felt lucky that this arrangement was permanent now and would stay that way. Knowledge that Kenny would recognize Susan's car, but not Joe's, continued to be a bit of a worry. So, when Joe bought a new car for himself, he gave his old one to Susan. Katie and Susan could, at last, go together anywhere they chose now and then, like the old days. Without fear of being followed.

* * *

In the beginning, Kenny suspected Katie was staying with Susan. He made call after call harassing her, hoping to catch her off guard and that she'd let information leak out. He used roundabout ways of trying to find out where Katie lived if it wasn't with her. Susan offered him nothing, finally having her phone number changed and replaced with an unlisted one. Kenny wouldn't be able to get it.

He gave up and began trying other means of discovering Katie's whereabouts.

He called the elementary school near Susan's home and asked if they could get a message to Marley Hagen. It took only a moment for him to receive word that no student with that name attended that school. That information was passed on to Katie from teachers she'd worked with in the past. He phoned Katie's place of employment using his best charm in trying to get her new home address. They refused to enlighten him. 'Someone' called again a few days later stating Katie had applied for a job with 'his firm' and asked questions about her that were not relevant. The Personnel Department, aware of her situation, declined comment, then advised Katie of these calls as a reminder to stay alert.

She believed that now, because Kenny had a new person in his life, he'd stop all those threats. The past problems would melt into bad memories. Certainly, she wouldn't change her activities for a while, but encouragement began to surface.

CHAPTER FIFTY-SIX

A vicious crack of lightening began at the top of the heavens and crashed to the ground. Its luminescence split the darkness in half before she could blink. The fat, scattered drops of rain were blown away and replaced with a treacherous downpour barely handled by the windshield wipers as they slapped back and forth with a fury across the glass. Katie's heart pounded. Her knuckles turned white and her wrists ached from the death-grip she had on the wheel.

She knew he had a huge advantage on her and could catch her any time he chose. Right now she was just his toy. Her rear view mirror let her know he'd pulled within a car's length of her. He stayed there, gradually inching closer to her bumper. Hovering like a vulture.

Sitting rigid in the seat, she looked straight ahead, not willing to give him the satisfaction of acknowledging she knew he'd found her and followed. Although unable to see his face she felt pretty sure of the maniacal smile on his mouth. The memory alone, of that smile, was frightening enough to make her stomach feel like turning inside out.

Apparently this encounter had been complete coincidence. Kenny seldom traveled this area, but Katie knew it well. She knew, that after spotting her, he'd flashed his headlights to put her on alert. To make his presence known. She felt he was likely gloating. She checked the mirror often and watched as he slowed down and backed off. Another burst of lightening illuminated his car clearly. Then the deluge increased and a wall of rain hid him from her clear view.

As the downpour eased she realized the dim lights in the distance behind her could belong to him or to someone else.

Continued glances in the mirror produced no comfort. For a full two or three minutes there was no sign she knew to be him. That was almost worse. At least she felt she had a chance when she knew where he was.

By being familiar with the surroundings, Katie knew she had a slight edge. Between deep breaths, she bit her lip to keep from crying and blurring her vision further. She sent her brain on a mental trip through the area searching for any place at all she might quickly turn into when Kenny was lagging behind.

She caught a flash of headlights flickering off and on that seemed half a block, or more, behind her. *Did I imagine that? Or was it just the rain diffusing the vision?*

The chase now headed toward the edge of town and she knew full well once they hit a rural region he would speed up and close in. She could only imagine which of his threats he'd select from the list of dozens he'd voiced over the years.

His quiver held many more arrows. Forcing her off the road, yank her from her car, tie her up and leave her there to die was only one he'd suggested. In this weather that would not be too hard to do.

In a rain-storm such as this one, other drivers would scurry past, anxious to get home. They'd never pay attention to cars stopped along the shoulder off the road. With vision impaired, it wasn't unusual for some drivers to do just that and wait for it to let up. No one would hear her scream over the thunder and lightening. Her only chance was to out-maneuver Kenny.

*I've got to stay cool. Think, dammit, think! Well, I'm in the lead. He's going to follow. I know this area. He doesn't. This time I'll give **him** something to wonder about.*

CHAPTER FIFTY-SEVEN

The rain refused to stop. It turned to a steady down-pour, but nothing like the pounding it had done for the past ten minutes. As the sadistic game continued, Katie, trembling and angry, formed a plan in her mind. *Can I make this work?*

She established a pattern of going up and down the streets, around one block then another, selecting turns at random and working her way closer to the edge of town. She believed Kenny thought he'd figured out her plan as he briefly dropped behind again and out of sight.

Katie chose this moment to make a left, going the wrong way on a one-way street heading back into town. She pushed the knob to turn off the headlights and sped forward. As she'd expected, the street was empty. To be stopped by a cop would be just fine with her. If not, just two more blocks and she'd be near the house where a friend, Linda, and her husband, lived.

She slipped into their driveway and around to the rear of their house finessing a spectacular escape. She knew they'd be happy to help. Sitting there in her car, hidden, proved to be a safety net. After a short wait, it was obvious she'd outsmarted him. What a feeling. Beautiful, sweet relief!

Lights inside the house were on, so she felt they were probably still up, watching TV or reading. Linda still taught at the same elementary school Katie once had. They'd often shared lunch breaks together, talking and becoming close enough that she offered a hiding place to Katie if it should ever come to that.

The rain slowed to a light drizzle. Lifting an umbrella from the floor, Katie opened the car door, raised the umbrella, and hurried around to the front of the house. After ringing the doorbell, she heard someone on the other side mumbling, surely wondering who stood at their door at eight o'clock at night and in this weather. Linda looked out through the peephole and, recognized Katie immediately as she stood under the porch light. She opened the door inviting Katie in.

Linda's husband thoughtfully disappeared into the den while Katie followed Linda into the kitchen. Within minutes, the two of them sat at the table sipping hot tea. As its calming warmth spread through her body Katie described the latest episode. Linda had trouble believing police couldn't help her. This was harassment at a minimum, threatening and stalking, maybe more, at the other end of the scale.

"I've gotten so I hate the damned cops," Katie said. "It always seems to end up being something they feel they shouldn't be involved in. That we are adults and should iron out our differences without their help. Do they ever read the newspaper?

Hardly a day goes by that someone isn't physically hurt by a mate. Then when someone murders his wife, they jump in and try to figure out why. How it might have been prevented. There's seldom any mention that she came to get protection, or help of some sort, from the police several times before they found her dead body. I just don't understand it."

Katie phoned Susan telling her she was with a friend in a safe haven, and that she'd be on the way home soon. Saying good-bye and thanks to Linda she headed out. Rain let up and the balance of the trip flowed without interruption.

When Katie got home she called Susan to let her know she'd arrived safely. Now Susan took Marley by the hand and the two of them walked across the damp back yards to where Katie waited.

Once Marley was tucked into bed for the night, Susan

listened to details about the frightening chase and narrow escape.

"Maybe you should look into getting a restraining order," said Susan.

"The trouble with that is that all of these incidents take place on public streets. I can't really prove a thing. I can't prove that he's trying to kill me. Or even hurt me. If I tried to do something he'd simply deny everything. I'm hoping he'll just get bored with it and stop if I refuse to take the bait."

CHAPTER FIFTY-EIGHT

Time to get rid of this car. It's more than seven years old now and wearing out. I know the trade-in won't be much, but there are two huge benefits: Kenny won't recognize me on the road, and I'll have a newer vehicle.

She recalled that used car dealers lined both sides of Route One. Now, driving around the area, the third place she stopped displayed a white, nineteen-eighty-seven, Ford Escort. Only three years old. The sign in the windshield read just under three thousand dollars. She could swing that. She went inside and asked about it.

"It's a real sweet little machine," the salesman assured her. "The price is right. They don't make 'em like that any more."

"I'd like to test drive it." Katie told him.

"No problem. Just let me just grab the keys from the office and we'll take her for a little spin."

He left. When he returned he handed the keys to Katie. Together they walked to the car. Katie slid in behind the wheel. Mr. No Problem took up his post on the passenger side. She inserted the key into the ignition when, to her dismay, she realized this was not an automatic transmission. It was a straight-stick.

Sheepishly she turned to Mr. No Problem and admitted, "I can't drive this. I've never driven anything but an automatic."

"No problem," said he. "I'll show you how. Just let me take her off the lot. There's a place right down the road where you can practice some."

By two o'clock she had good understanding of the basics,

talked the price down more than she believed she could, and began the drive home in a newer car.

She stalled out at a couple of traffic lights. Restarting it, the car lurched forward spastically. It would definitely take a while to get used to a clutch.

CHAPTER FIFTY-NINE

She lifted the receiver to her ear. "Hello."

"Hey, Katie." A pause. "This ish Elwood. How'r you?"

"Hi, Elwood." She waited, mentally filtering the possible reasons for the call. "I'm doing fine. I haven't talked to you in a year. What have you been up to? Are you okay? You sound…um… a little drunk. "

"I've had a couple beers, but no, I'm not drunk. I'm okay here. Hanging 'round with Kenny, you know. Not doing a lot. Just like always. You know he sold the house?"

"Well, I'm really curious. Why are you calling? And how did you get my number?"

The divorce was final over a year ago. She hadn't talked to him or seen him since. She felt no need to change that. She liked Elwood, but where Elwood was, Kenny would not be far behind. A package deal. They'd been friends for years.

Katie noticed that he waited a moment before answering, as though he needed to find the right words. To get the point across without her hanging up on him?

"You know he sold the house?" he repeated.

"I thought he probably would. That's fine with me. I have a fresh start. He needs the same."

"He's got a little place out in the country now. An acre of land. Lots of trees and stuff. It's quiet and peaceful there. You'd love it."

"Sounds good, Elwood, but not for me."

"Katie, Kenny needs to see you. He's really in a bad way and I'm worried about him. He keeps asking for you."

"Elwood, I'm sorry he's in a bad way, whatever that might be, but you know, that's not my problem. I don't trust him. I have no idea where that new place is, and I'll never put myself *anywhere* alone with him. Especially out in the country somewhere."

"I can tell you how to get here. It's easy. If you come over, I'll stay while you're here. I know he used to be mean to you. Threaten you and all. But he's in no shape to hurt you now. And I don't think he even wants to any more. He should see some kind of doctor. Find out what's wrong with him. Maybe you could talk him into going."

"You talk to him, Elwood. I have nothing to say to him."

"He needs you, Katie."

"He didn't listen to me then, he won't listen to me now. We're apart and it's working just fine. It's permanent, you know. He offers nothing and, although I could, maybe even should, I ask for nothing. It's just better that we are out of each other's lives."

"You know he never wanted the divorce. He's been going downhill ever since you two split up for good. Katie, you know he's had a quick temper. He might have settled down some lately. Can you come over for a little while? Just talk to him?"

"No, Elwood, I can't. My life is peaceful now. No need to stir up old unpleasant business."

"Well, at least think about it. I'll call you again tomorrow. It's Saturday and won't interfere with your work or anything. I'll stay here for you. Just give it some thought. Okay?"

"Well, you can call if you like, but I'm quite sure I won't change my mind."

"Thanks, Katie. Talk tomorrow, then. Bye." An abrupt hang-up.

* * *

Elwood's call kept replaying in Katie's head. Although he'd said Kenny needed her, she didn't want to see him. Didn't even want to talk to him. He'd finally left her alone. Basking in that relief, now she wished him no harm, just to stay out of her life. But would Elwood call if this weren't really important? Still, she'd told him no. She'd stick to it.

As predicted, Elwood called the next day, repeating his promise to protect her and not to let things get out of hand. "Maybe if you and I, together, figure out a plan, Kenny will listen," he said.

She didn't stick to what she'd said the day before. She trusted Elwood. Katie caved. She'd go see if she could help.

CHAPTER SIXTY

Following Elwood's directions she located the small frame structure he'd described, set back off the road, nestled among dozens of trees. Very well hidden, if one didn't know what to look for. No sooner had she clicked the ignition off than Elwood appeared by the car door, opening it for her. She got out wondering if he'd been watching out a front window while she maneuvered her car down the long dirt driveway.

"Thanks, Katie." He hugged her. "I'm glad you changed your mind. Have any trouble finding the place?"

"No. The directions you gave were perfect. Elwood, you do need to know that I won't be staying long, though. I'm hoping the two of us can figure out a way to convince him to do something, whatever it may be, to get his health and life back on track."

"I told him you'd be here."

"Elwood, I'm really here for you as much, or more than, for him. You need each other. The two of you have been best buddies for years and years. In spite of his craziness you've always stood by him. You are a very special kind of friend."

"Thanks. We don't always agree, but he's treated me pretty well. As for me, I always try to keep his head straight. But after his mom and dad were killed in that crash a year ago I've felt a need to help him even more through his rough times. Seems like I can't do it all on my own, though."

"Yeah, both parents at once. That was sad. He'd never been really close with them. But, my god, that had to be tough to take."

"Well, let's go inside. I'll let him know you're here."

CHAPTER SIXTY-ONE

The dismal appearance of the interior of the small house proved more disheartening than she could have imagined. The living room was nearly bare. A fresh coat of paint would improve the walls. Anything other than beige. Something with some color to brighten it.

Katie felt her current thought might be a bit perverted, but it brought an inward smile nonetheless as she remembered "Goddammit, Katie, no *man* wants a *pink* living room." from Kenny years ago. *Maybe I should come here sometime, when no one's around, and paint it pink.*

Odds and ends of furniture looked as though all of it had been dropped from above and left to sit wherever and however it landed on the floor. Both of the front windows were covered with heavy drapes, refusing to admit the sun. An oval, threadbare rug covered the center of the floor. The television was on. No one watched it. It droned on: a low, monotonous, weary sound that sounded depressing. Elwood went over and clicked it off.

Surveying the surroundings further, Katie couldn't help but notice the familiar number of beer cans perched on a coffee table. Several more decorated the floor. The room fairly stank. It reeked like a cheap bar the morning after New Year's Eve. *Some things never change.*

At least those crumpled fast food wrappers scattered around add some color to the place.

"Hey, Kates."

Jumping involuntarily, she turned to see Kenny standing close behind her.

"How ya doin'?"

"Hi, Kenny. I'm doing well, thanks."

"Glad you stopped in to pay a visit. Not quite like our old place I've got here, huh?"

Ignoring the nature of that comment she said, "It could be worse. Looks like you have everything you need."

"Well, at least it keeps the rain out." A weird smile crawled across his lips. "Here, let me show ya 'round." He reached his hand out to her. The repulsive odor of stale beer seemed to be suspended in the air surrounding him, following him as he moved. It wasn't yet noon.

Refusing to acknowledge the gesture of his out-reached hand, she lowered herself onto the sofa. "Let's just sit and talk a bit. Elwood called to tell me you haven't been feeling well. I came here to help him to help you."

"Yeah, Elwood's a good guy. My best buddy." He turned to look at his friend. "Ain't ya, Elwood?"

For a moment no one spoke.

Then, to Katie: "Ya heard 'bout my folks?"

"Yes, it was in the newspaper. Must have been very difficult for you."

"Yeah, but losing you was worse." He slumped onto the sofa.

"Kenny, please. Let's don't go there."

"Okay, not now, anyway." It took some effort, but he managed to stand again.

"How about a bite to eat?"

Facing his buddy he said, "Elwood, take the car and go on up to that little restaurant and grab some lunch for all of us, will ya?"

Elwood faltered a bit before answering. "Uh, sure, Kenny."

"Kenny, you know I didn't come for lunch. I'm really not hungry." Katie said.

"Just trying to be a gracious host, here." He picked up a can of warm beer off the floor, draining what remained inside. "Elwood, go on. Go get us somethin' tasty." He fished into a pocket of his jeans and pulled out a few twenties. Handing them to Elwood, he said, "Go on now. Get us somthin' good."

The two men stared at each other, almost challenging. The air crackled with tension.

"Kenny, I promised our wife I'd hang around."

"*Our* wife?"

"Uh, no. That was a slip. A mistake. Not what I meant at all. *Your* wife."

Listening to this, Katie wondered which would burst open first, her heart or her head. Trying to smooth things over she said, "Ex-wife, would say it best."

The room fell silent as a grave.

CHAPTER SIXTY-TWO

Katie reacted first, a valiant effort of attempting to create a normalcy around the three of them. "Well, looks like I came at a bad time. Guess I'll head on out. We'll catch up another day."

"Nah, sit right there and make yourself comfy. Elwood will bring us some lunch back, won'tcha, Elwood? We can start right, all over again."

"Uh, sure. I'll get some burgers and fries. Maybe even a chocolate shake for you, Katie. I remember how that used to be a rare treat for you." He inched toward the door. "I'll be back real soon."

Although he closed the door behind him quietly as he left, Katie felt he'd abandoned her. He may as well slammed it shut. He'd promised to stay!

Regaining composure, Katie stood. A sense of desperation wrapped around her, a warning that she, alone, now held the responsibility to protect herself.

"Really, Kenny, I think I should go. This turned out to be not such a good idea."

"Nah, we don't need to wait for Elwood. Let's us just go ahead and start over now."

He flopped onto the sofa. Patting the cushion next to his with his hand, he encouraged, "Sit on down here a-side me, Kates. Up close so we can really talk."

Her handbag still lay there. Reaching for it she said, "No, Kenny. I'm leaving. And really, you don't look sick like Elwood told me you were."

He gripped her wrist, pulling her off her feet, forcing her to land on the sofa near him.

"I'm sick in my heart, Kates."

Struggling to keep an even tone in her voice, and not broadcast her mounting fears, she said, "Let go of my wrist, Kenny." She made a move to get up. He tightened his hold.

"Kenny," she pleaded, "this isn't part of the deal. I want to leave. Turn me loose. If you *are* sick, you're sick in the head, not the heart. I don't believe you even have a heart."

Katie managed to jerk to her feet. Kenny, right behind her, realized he'd nearly lost his grip on her wrist. In one swift motion he reinforced his control, twisting her arm up and behind her back. With her free hand she swung a fist at him, making little contact. He laughed at her.

"Ya still a feisty little bitch, ain't ya?"

He stood in back of her nudging her along, heading deeper into another part of the house.

Attempting to slam her heel into his crotch she swung her foot up behind her. That, too, missed the mark. The extra twist he applied to her arm made her scream. He slapped his other hand over her mouth.

A wild laugh burst from his mouth. "Ain't nobody gonna hear ya, city girl. Ya in the country now." That laughter belonged to the devil itself.

He dropped his hand from across her face, and used it to shove her into the bedroom.

"Kenny, stop! You're really hurting my arm!"

Relaxing his hold was all the opportunity she needed. She broke free. Turning toward him she kicked at him. Both her arms whirled toward any place on his body they might make contact.

A single punch to her stomach dropped her to her knees. Rather than trying to stand, crawling to the door they'd just come through seemed to be the only way to escape. He grabbed hold of her hair, pulling upward. The pain insisted that she stand.

Once upright, hate and fury spread through her like a forest fire. He still held a handful of her hair. Taking another swing might prove to be her biggest mistake yet. But what she said next might cost her her life.

"I know about Lizzie."

CHAPTER SIXTY-THREE

For a while a single sound penetrated her ears: her own heartbeat. She saw a look of dazed bewilderment sweep across Kenny's face. Katie watched in disbelief as Kenny's hands fell to his sides. Both arms seemed fragile as they dangled from his shoulders. They looked lightweight, as though they were made of tissue paper and had no muscle beneath the skin. His face appeared like a wax reproduction of the Kenny she knew a lifetime ago. But now, that wax seemed to be melting. The illusion stopped and the oddly shaped features remained frozen into a grotesque mask. His lips moved. But no sound came out. A full minute passed. He attempted to speak once more.

Then a sudden howl, "What do ya know?" roared from his mouth. It produced the haunting sound of hurricane wind and rain as it rushed over gravel, finally being swallowed up as it whirled down the storm drain. Gutteral and raw.

"What do ya know?" he growled.

Unable to speak, Katie stared at him. Stunned, she watched as his complete appearance looked to be transforming into a comic strip character. Still, she offered no response.

Then, *"Answer me! What do ya know?"* Kenny's voice was close to a screech.

She filtered thoughts as an assortment of words bounced around in her head. Adrenaline coursed through her system. Katie stood tall now, feeling a new surge of power as Kenny continued to unravel while he confused illusion with reality. Her reply was deliberate and slow. Low and level and even, she enunciated clearly.

"I know you killed her. And I know how."

This mistake obscured others she'd made today. Maybe any she'd *ever* made. Too late it dawned on her that the accusation was only a guess. She knew nothing. That statement had been thrown out as a possible weapon to hold over his head. As some perceived knowledge. It was a contrived move on her part. She'd felt that might urge him to bargain with her rather than continue physical abuse.

His arms reached out toward Katie. He caught her, pulled her close and curled both hands around her neck. He squeezed. Her lungs begged for oxygen. They silently screamed for just a breath. Aching for air erased her energy, eliminating any ability to fight. The more she tried to move and twist, the tighter his fingers clutched. Then tighter. Katie fell limp. Darkness enveloped her.

CHAPTER SIXTTY-FOUR

Kenny lifted her roughly. She aroused for a moment as he tossed her over his shoulder and carried her the final few steps to the bed. Both her shoes dropped to the floor along the way. After dumping her onto the mattress he secured each of her wrists to the metal bed frame. He unbuckled the belt from his jeans and used it around one wrist. *Ha! Just what ya get for messing with me.* On the other, the silk necktie he still owned from their wedding so long ago. *Remember this tie, Katie?* His smile oozed revenge. *You picked it out. I never wear a goddam tie. But it's perfect for you.* The tie seemed incredibly appropriate to him.

Spending such physical and mental energy produced a gradual sobering effect on him. He lit a cigarette then sat on the edge of the mattress watching Katie. She stirred. He wondered whether she might regain consciousness. After convincing himself that it didn't matter much one way or the other, he decided to have one final sexual adventure with her body.

Kenny unzipped her jeans. Slipping them, and a pair of pink lacy panties off her torso together, he flung both across the room. He thought she might be coming to. Waking up. His fingers circled her neck again. They tightened. *No, not yet. Maybe not at all. You're mine forever now.*

His own Levi's and Jockey shorts slid to his ankles and were allowed to rest where he stepped out of them.

Looking at the nude lower half of Katie's body Kenny felt one conflicting emotion after another: love, hate; desire, disgust; curiosity, indifference; fear, comfort; fear, danger; then fear again. At last he positioned his body atop hers. Moving with careful deliberation he felt determined to achieve an erection. Nothing happened. Yet, he continued in slow motion. He'd take his time. There was no hurry.

Katie felt short puffs of air work their way into her lungs, beginning a painful recovery from the near-fatal choking. She coughed and sputtered, desperate for breath. She knew that should have sent an alarm to Kenny, but she couldn't hold it back. She also had no doubt that he'd tuned out and heard nothing but the noises in his own head.

Katie realized what he was trying to do, and that he'd tied down her arms. With no strength left for fighting, she knew she couldn't fend off another attack. She kept her eyes closed and remained statue still, evaluating the situation and tried to figure out how she might be able to save herself. She was sober. He was drunk. But he was unfettered while she was attached to the bed frame. Although, terror and urgency to escape continued to rule her thoughts, it also fueled a desire to humiliate Kenny. She deserved some revenge.

Yielding to yet another phenomenally bad idea, she blurted, "So, you can't get it up any more, huh?"

As she spoke he smashed his fist into her jaw. She screamed.

The front door opened.

CHAPTER SIXTY-FIVE

"Hey, guys, I've got lunch. Where are you?"

Katie twisted, trying to get up, hoping help had arrived. Kenny, covered Katie's mouth with his paw, and yelled, "I'll be out in a minute."

Elwood had already rounded the corner and stood digesting the scene before him: Kenny, half naked, sprawled on top of Katie. And that her wrists were bound to the bed.

"Kenny, what the fuck you doing?" he boomed. Dropping the food where he stood, he rushed at Kenny. Pulling him off Katie, the two men wrestled to the floor. When they got up Elwood yelled again. "You promised you wouldn't hurt her! You swore! You gave your word! What the hell is the matter with you? Untie her! Turn her loose!"

"Ain't none-a yer business, man." Kenny told Elwood.

"Yeah, *now* it is! I'm undoing her wrists."

"Don't touch her. She ain't yers."

"Go to hell." He calmly removed the leather belt and the silk tie, throwing both at Kenny. He grabbed a blanket off the floor and spread it over Katie. "Katie, I'm so sorry," he whispered. "I had no idea."

Acknowledging defeat, Kenny shrugged his shoulders and lit a cigarette. He flopped back onto the edge of the bed again, one hand on Katie's knee, daring her to move. A minute passed. Then another. Time was frozen.

* * *

"Pick that crap up off the floor," Kenny demanded. He stood

and lumbered toward the kitchen.

He returned with a cold six-pack in one hand, an open beer in the other, another cigarette dangling from his lips. "Let's have a little lunch now, what ya think? Elwood went to all that trouble. We should eat."

"No one has much of an appetite right now," Katie said.

"I ain't askin', I'm tellin'. Have a burger and a shake."

"The shake spilled all over the floor," said Katie. "Don't believe I'll lick it up."

Kenny opened his third beer in the past few minutes. Katie watched as his eyes shrunk into slits. She thought he looked shrewd. Cagey enough to create a scheme.

"Elwood, *my buddy,* I think ya screwed up royally this time. I want ya the hell outta the house. Don't even think I want ya to come back again. Ever."

"Great, Kenny," said Katie. " Elwood is the only friend you have left. Probably the only one you'll ever have. You could be a little nicer to him."

"I don't gotta be nice to him," Kenny yelled. "He's an asshole!"

The words and punches between the men began again. Pummeling each other they tumbled back and forth on the floor until they were exhausted and panting. Katie stayed out of it and kept quiet, biding her time, trying, finally, to play it smart.

Both men took a break to consume more beer. Then, fired up all over again, Kenny started yelling. "Elwood, get the hell outta here. This is my house. Ya ain't no friend no more."

"I ain't leaving. I don't like the way you're treatin' Katie. She don't deserve that."

Kenny stood up, wobbling toward Elwood. Lunging at him. Pushing him to the floor. Elwood's fingers wrapped around Kenny's ankle bringing him down with a thud. They wrestled like maniacs til Kenny's hand caught an empty bottle that had rolled out from under the bed. He swung it at Elwood's head. Elwood jumped up and backed off. Fists he could handle, but weapons weren't part of this fight.

"Get the fuck outta here I said! I never wanna see ya again. Ya go *now*, else I'll git my rifle and make ya dance all the way out the door." He stood and stumbled toward the closet where he kept the rifle.

Elwood bolted. Katie felt betrayed. She knew from now on she was on her own.

* * *

Figuring Kenny to be close to collapsing into a drunken stupor, Katie remained on the bed pretending to be asleep. She knew any movement from her and he'd be ready to come at her again. She must be quiet. And still. No escape plan came to mind. But she knew she needed extra patience to be successful with anything she might come up with. A quick, creative escape was crucial.

Katie continued to watch as Kenny sat on the opposite edge of the bed mumbling to himself. He kept drinking beer and lighting one cigarette from the end of another. Katie wondered why he studied the ribbon of smoke as it curled upward. He seemed entranced by it. This made her realise that his mind had slipped into another universe and that all thoughts he'd had of her had evaporated.

As she'd predicted, he passed out soon and toppled over on the bed, still clutching a lit cigarette between his fingers. Katie decided against taking it away from him and wondered if other butts smoldered in the sheets. She would leave it be.

Throughout, believing her very life was at stake, Katie struggled to stay quiet and alert, sensing the odds would ultimately shift balance to her favor. After what seemed like an eternity, the suggestion of possible safety presented itself. Still terrified of the probable results if Kenny should make a quick recovery, she slipped out of the bed and scurried across the floor. She picked up her panties and jeans and pulled them on. As she rushed to leave she grabbed her handbag and stepped into her shoes moving as fast as she was able.

Silently exiting the house, Katie deliberately dismissed the smell of burning fabric. Hurrying to her car, she thought she caught a glimpse of Elwood crouched down by the bushes near the house. *Is that really Elwood? Well, screw him, too. I'm done with them both.*

At last speeding away from danger, she now felt sure the entire thing had been a ploy to reunite her with Kenny. How could she have fallen into such an obvious trap?

CHAPTER SIXTY-SIX

Susan and Katie sat in lawn chairs and watched as Marley practiced riding her bike along the worn pathway in the back yard.

"What are you going to do?" Susan asked.

"I'm not sure. Going to the police hasn't been any help in the past. They keep brushing me off. Insisting it's nothing they'll get involved in. Domestic issues, they tell me. Solve them on your own."

"Well, this is a bit different, don't you think?"

"It is, I know. I'm a nervous wreck over it. When I think how close I came to dying. Being killed, actually, I start to fall apart. I have no idea how I managed to stay even a little calm during all that. I sure don't feel any of that calmness now."

"Katie, you did what you had to do. Somehow something inside kicked into high gear and your only thought was survival. That wasn't the time to fall apart. Now, though, it's okay. You're home and safe."

"Thanks, I know you're right. A lot of it seems like a bad dream, but I know how real it was and it still has the power to make me shake."

"And you've heard nothing from either of them?"

"Not a word. And I'm sure I won't. Their little plan didn't work out so well for them."

"What if Kenny starts up with his old 'tricks' again? What will you do then?"

"Honestly, Susan, if that happens I may get a gun and learn

how to shoot it. I can't live the rest of my life with this fear."

They sat lost in thought for a few minutes, weighing the possibilities of a peaceful life. And what might be done to achieve it.

A commotion broke their reverie. Noticing several vehicles moving down the street near Katie's house they both rose to their feet.

"I'd better go see what's going on out there," said Katie.

"I'll come with you."

Katie recognized one car as she got to the corner of the yard. She turned to Susan.

"Susan, it's the police. It looks like they might be stopping here. Will you take Marley to your house? She doesn't need to be around this. Keep her there. I'll call you later."

Susan took Marley's hand. "Marley, come to my house for lunch. I'll fix something special."

Susan and Marley walked across the back lawn. Katie turned and climbed the stairs leading from the back yard into her house. From where she stood she heard the doorbell ring.

* * *

Her heart pounded with violence. The police? Yes, at her door. Of course the news wasn't going to be good. She took a step forward. Her knees buckled but she managed to catch hold of the railing and keep from falling.

The bell rang a second time.

"Hang on, I'm coming," Katie called out and did her best to

hurry through the house to open the front door.

Two uniformed men waited, but watched over her shoulders to determine whether someone else was in the room with her. One spoke.

"Mrs. Hagen? Katie Hagen?"

"Yes."

"Open up. We need to come in."

She backed up and they stepped inside. One removed handcuffs from the back of his belt and took hold of Katie's arm. The other officer produced a paper as he announced, "We have a warrant for your arrest."

"A warrant? For my arrest? For what?"

"For the murder of one Kenneth Hagen."

"What!?"

He pulled her arms behind her back and clasped the cuffs around both wrists. So began the routine litany: "you have the right to remain silent…"

They guided her out the door supporting her as she stumbled between them in shock. Television and newspaper reporters had already arrived and hovered like vultures. They asked questions, digging into the story as it unfolded. All of them talked at her at once as they shoved a microphone toward her heckling for any sort of a response. Katie held her head high, looking straight ahead, and refused to be goaded into any of it. Although a crowd of neighbors had assembled she reminded herself she'd been in more difficult situations than this one.

Little time elapsed before live television aired it. They

broadcast the event with a dramatic flair. More so than usual news, because this was a female whom they believed committed murder. This was certainly something you didn't hear about often. They contrived all sort of possible motives leaving it to the public to decide what to believe.

The reporters played with their own imaginations, twisting every small item, trying to pick up something they could use to intrigue their audiences, hinting they knew answers that no one else did.

* * *

Her first call, of course, was to Susan. After all, Marley was with Susan. She promised to take care of her as long as Katie couldn't. And with genuine friendship, going above and beyond the call, she assured Katie that Joe would find an attorney to handle the case.

The story and Katie's picture, as she was being fingerprinted, took up the top third of the next morning's paper. She sat in a jail cell, arrested for murder. Now what?

CHAPTER SIXTY-SEVEN

As Katie gave tremendous effort to become acclimated to living conditions she'd never imagined, the most difficult of all was how she missed Marley. The profound emptiness and sorrow that were inside her brought tears and frustration on a regular basis. Even so, in the beginning she refused to allow Susan to bring Marley to visit.

In addition, being unable to connect, on any level, with anyone else detained there, Katie felt wounded and withdrew into herself. As days crawled by she finally met with Mr. Webster, the attorney Joe had sent to see her. Although not overly impressed with him she learned he was one of a team of criminal lawyers who would be involved in her defense.

Still no trial date had been set. Boredom was beyond measure. With so little to do Katie requested library privileges. She still needed something else to help pass the time. Warden Janetta Wilsky let her know she could schedule time in the gym if she felt some exercise might be helpful.

For some reason Katie and Wilksy had clicked immediately. When the 'resident' count was low, and days dragged, conversation between the two women grew from polite to friendly – a surprise to both of them. Little by little each divulged tidbits about their youth. Their earlier life. How they arrived at their current place. They developed a mutual understanding and respect.

* * *

A year of invasive monotony ran its course. Katie remained in jail tormented by what brought her there. She still felt the intense grief of missing her only child. *I need to get out of here. Susan and Joe won't be able to take care of Marley forever. She*

212

might have to go into some sort of facility provided by the state. Then maybe foster parents. That's not the life I want for her.

* * *

Wilsky stopped at Katie's cage.

"Want to talk about it?" she asked.

"Talk about what?"

"What got you here."

"Not much to say, really. I didn't kill the bastard, although maybe I should have."

"Well, someone thinks you did. Actually, a lot of someone's."

"Yeah, so I've heard,"

"What was he like? What happened?"

"Hey, you know you won't get a confession out of me."

"Ahh, I'm not angling for any confession. I'm just curious as to how you got so tangled up."

"Yeah, sorry. Somehow I believe you."

"Well, feel free. It's all off the record. And I promise I'm not wired up, if that's a worry to you."

"For months now I really have been trying to sort out this whole mess in my mind. My mind just won't cooperate lately, though. Maybe another time," Katie said.

"Okay. I'll offer you the 'installment plan of talking'. A little one day, and a little another day. However it might work for you."

"I'll think about it. That doesn't sound so bad."

* * *

After another fitful night of bad dreams Katie awoke crying. She remembered waking up happy or angry many times in her life, but never crying. She heard the early daytime noises around her and decided just a cup of coffee would do this morning. Those who went to breakfast would be chattering and making a lot of noise about things she didn't care a bit about. Her head was full of memories. She needed to wade through them and concentrate on the future. The jumble of thoughts rushed her back into time. She didn't want to go there, but maybe it was necessary.

*What's the matter with me? Where was my brain all these years? His angry outbursts. His threats. How he seemed to enjoy the terror he caused. I was stupid enough to defend him—even to myself. I wanted to believe him. Believe **in** him. In us.*

*Excusing him, I blamed myself for things I had nothing to do with. Always thinking there were no signs of anger building or problems developing. Dammit! There **were** signs. The little ones I guess I don't remember, but there were others I should have paid serious attention to.*

Wilsky walked down the row doing the morning body check nodding at Katie as she passed. Once that was done she worked her way back to Katie.

"How's it going?" Wilsky asked.

"Ahh, not great."

"What's up?"

"Oh, I just had a rough night and woke up in a worse mood than usual."

"Feel like talking?"

"You going to play shrink today?" Katie asked.

"Sure. Can't hurt. Sometimes two brains work better than one."

"My head was flooded with memories from years ago. I actually woke up crying. How's that for a start?"

"Better that most. And more truthful than many, as well. You want to keep going? I have some time, so pour it out. I can take it. After all these years, I'm a pretty fair judge of people. Much of what they've written about you, I've had trouble believing. I'm thinking he was a real sonofabitch. Of course, I could be wrong." She leaned against the barred wall of the cage.

CHAPTER SIXTY-EIGHT

Katie hesitated. Then began

"There are so many, um, coincidences. I remember, early on, when I still lived off-campus in my parent's house and I often saw a blue car drive slowly by. At first I was flattered, but then always afraid to ask; now I'm sure it was him. Checking up? Stalking? I don't know.

More than a year after that we got married. Then that winter, right after the snowfall, I fell at the parking lot of the A & P. What do you think is the last car I remember seeing? The one that turned down the lane where I'd parked. The blue one that looked like it wanted to run over me. And nearly did. I had to jump out of the way. When I landed I broke my leg. Was it Kenny? Certainly could have been. I'd never have believed it then, but today I'd bet money on it."

"Did you ever question him about any of it?"

"No. I was young and dumb. Well, not dumb, but I knew little about men. And I didn't want to believe he would do anything like that. I mean, really, we were married!"

They grew quiet, letting those thoughts sink in and settle down before more were piled on top of them.

Wilsky spoke first.

"So you weren't so good at recognizing a vehicle by its name – only by a color. Did things like that happen often?"

"Sporadically, I suppose. Not many that big. But he did have a temper. And, truly Wilsky, the only thing I can be positive in of in that incident is the blue car. But he gave no warning signs that I could detect."

"But he always seemed to know where you'd be? How did that happen?"

"Well, when Susan and I went out to lunch we usually requested a table by a window. Especially if the weather was pleasant. We're both people-watchers. Kenny always asked for details about where we'd be going and I'd tell him. No reason not to. Both Susan and I often saw a blue car drive slowly by the restaurant. Each of us, for a long time, too uncomfortable about the possibilities to mention it to the other. Kenny? Maybe. I'll never know for sure."

"Katie, I'm seeing a pattern develop here. You had no idea?"

"There are hundreds of blue cars on the road. Once in a while I'd wonder for a minute, but then it seemed too silly so the thought just vanished."

"Did he have any friends? Could he have been jealous of your friends? Did he trust you?"

"He had some friends. Well, more like acquaintances, not really friends. They'd come by and play cards now and then but they never went out anywhere. His only true friend was Elwood. They'd been tight since elementary school. He was at the house a lot. He and I got along well, too. He behaved like a gentleman. I liked him.

"I know a lot of what I'm saying is coming out disjointed. Guess I'm giving you highlights more than a lot of detail. Sorry."

"That's okay. When it pops into your head say it. Something important might be uncovered. Go on about some of the other things that happened. Maybe we can figure out something to help your lawyers. They don't come around much to see you. How will they know what you've been through if they don't come and talk to you? They'll be scheduling the trial soon."

"I know. I just feel like I'm rotting away in here. And I miss my Marley so much I don't know what to do." Tears welled up in Katie's eyes. Holding them back became an impossible chore.

"Okay. I'm done with this. At least for now. Maybe we'll continue another time," she turned her back on Wilsky.

For a moment Wilsky stood there. Then she ambled on down the row and back to her desk to take care of paperwork that had piled up. Katie had given her plenty to try to sort out.

CHAPTER SIXTY-NINE

Katie thought about her future and slipped deeper into a funk as another week crawled by. For days afterward there were no more 'sessions' between Katie and Wilksy.

"Any time you're ready for a re-match let me know," Wilsky said.

"A re-match?"

"Yeah, I hung my shingle out again."

"Oh. Sorry, I didn't pick up on that at first. My mind must be somewhere else. So, you have a need to hear me complain some more?"

Wilsky laughed. "Nah, complaining isn't what I'd call it."

"What, then?"

"I feel like we are searching for answers and information to feed your lawyer. And I've got to admit I'm curious as well. So many things don't make sense."

"Give me another couple of days, maybe I'll be ready.

"Okay, Monday then. This is Thursday. I'll let you have the weekend off." Wilsky laughed and tapped the bars with the magazine she held in her hand and walked on.

Katie slumped on the cot and let her memories take her back in time again.

The brakes on the Pinto stopped working right after Susan and I returned from a week at the beach. He had all week to make that happen. Did he do it? The suggestion the tow truck driver gave should have made me wonder. Kenny was indignant when I told him about it. Angry over just a casual suggestion. He had time to do it. Now, I believe he did.

* * *

On Monday Wilsky stopped at Katie's cell at the end of her morning check. Her eyes held a twinkle.

"Do you need an appointment?" she asked.

"How does your schedule look today?"

"This afternoon is clear. Several of the thirty-day-regulars will be leaving so I'll have some time before they bring the new ones in. That's all most of them get. In and out like a noisy cheap hotel. It's quite a life they lead. I'll come back later if you're ready to get into this again."

"My head has been crammed with things that happened. There were many arguments that seemed way over the top. But our being together wasn't <u>all</u> bad. We had some good times. Ultimately, the bad outweighed everything else.

So, yes, come on back when you have the time. I'm not going anywhere. Maybe something helpful will rise to the top."

"Okay. I'll see you this afternoon, then."

* * *

When Wilsky returned the two of them settled in for some serious conversation. Katie had an uphill battle ahead of her and both felt that talking aloud about past events might help her through it. Maybe something forgotten would be remembered. And be useful.

So they began with Katie offering a litany of disturbing memories. She described in detail many of the things that led to

220

the divorce, working up to the major one.

"I overheard his conversation with Elwood. Kenny was talking about a shovel. About killing me and Marley. *Killing* us! Burying us by the garage. And a shiny new shovel appeared in the garage a few days later. That was surely the beginning of the end."

"That had to scare the hell out of you. What did you do about it?"

"I went to the police. They blew me off, saying they didn't get involved in domestic issues. We needed to solve it ourselves. They were completely useless."

"Did you question Kenny?"

"Yeah. After I'd seen the shovel and been to the police. He told me he'd bought it for me to use in the garden. Can you believe he had the nerve to say something like that? I had no use for a shovel that size. And he knew it."

"So you really believed he had 'plans' to use it himself?"

"Yes, but not in the garden. I was scared enough for Marley and myself that I made immediate arrangements to get out of there. I couldn't possibly live there with him under those conditions and with that fear hanging over me all the time."

"Smart move. So you decided to divorce him? And move out?"

"I did. Once that began, the terrifying car chases did, too. A danger level beyond anything I could have imagined. To have your life threatened constantly, with no resources to counteract it, seemed like all-out war."

"The guy was destroying you."

"He sure tried. So now we have come to this. Kenny's death has been ruled a homicide. Elwood, the only hope I have for an eye-witness to back up my story, is still missing. He may be mourning. I couldn't blame him. He may have gone into hiding. They'd been best friends since grade school. And since I've been accused of Kenny's murder I've spent two years in jail. I think if he was going to show up and be of some help he would have done it long before now. So he's bailed out and won't protect me like he promised.

"I guess you've heard the trial has been scheduled? Only two months from now. It will bring all the ugly stuff out in the open. Going through it the first time scared me out of my wits. Constant threats on your life can do that. This, though, will be worse, but in a different way because it is so public. My waiting game continues.

"Marley is staying with Susan and Joe. They love her and are still taking care of her. But for how much longer?

"My parents are still somewhere in Europe, not that they might offer any help. But I keep thinking if they come back home they might decide to take Marley. I'm not sure they would, but I don't want them to raise her. If something happens with Susan and Joe what will become of her?"

CHAPTER SEVENTY

"Ladies and gentlemen of the jury. Take a good look at the woman sitting there at the defense table. She's attractive, isn't she? Perfect make-up. Not a hair out of place. And dressed up for the occasion. She looks like someone you might see in any of the nicer places. Maybe even on the cover of a fashion magazine.

"She's an intelligent woman, she attended college on a scholarship. Now a mom, with an eight-year-old daughter. That's a pleasant picture. The proper up-scale ingredients are there.

"There's only one glitch: with all that's going for her she doesn't have a husband. Well, she *did*. But now, folks, turns out that it's not such a pretty picture after all. Here's the punch line: she's a murderer. She killed the husband, She did it viciously and in cold blood.

"During this trial I'll tell you the details. The how and when and the where. It was ugly. It was brutal. Don't let her appearance fool you."

* * *

Next the defense attorney stepped up.

"Good morning folks. My name is Mr. Webster. I'm proud to be the attorney for Mrs. Hagen. Katie. The prosecution is already beginning to fill your heads with fabricated information. Stories they have made up. He will be trying his best to convince you that this young woman committed murder. That she killed her ex-husband.

"How he will do that I have no idea. Each piece of the so-called evidence that he tosses your way will be flimsy. He'll toss them to the wall to see what sticks. After he tosses them your way I suggest you toss them, too. Into the trash. He has not one shred of anything concrete. Weak circumstantial possibilities are the best he has to offer. Certainly nothing that would convict Katie Hagen, of murder.

"Did she have a motive? Absolutely. More than one. There were many occasions that her life and that of their daughter were threatened by her ex-husband.

"If you have children surely you'll understand the rage you'd feel if anyone, even your mate, let you know that child would be in true danger at his or her hand. Seems likely that motive existed.

"Did she have opportunity? That, too, is freely admitted. She was coerced by his best friend to come help him convince Mr. Hagen to seek medical help. That friend had promised to intervene if physical harm looked likely. When the friend should have jumped in to help, he bolted instead, leaving her to design and complete a way to escape being seriously hurt or killed by her ex-husband.

"Katie's a nice person who ended up being the victim in an abusive marriage. Through divorce, she had saved herself and her little girl from further danger and had moved on with her life. Even so, she felt that helping him–the abusive ex-husband mind you. to get on with his own life was the honorable thing to do. So against her better judgment she went to see him.

"While she was there he attacked her, causing her both bodily and emotional harm. When she was able to escape to go back home, he was still alive.

"Pay attention to what the prosecutor tells you. He's trying very hard to put a puzzle together. You'll see the pieces just don't fit. They were made by different companies. If you understand what went on, and what's real and what isn't you will find her not guilty. It will be an easy decision. She simply didn't do it."

* * *

By the time the opening arguments were over and the trial started, it had gained notoriety. The public had waited over two years for the trial to finally begin. Now, noisy crowds waited outside for the Courthouse doors to open hoping to get a front row seat on a bench. From the beginning the prosecutor was brutal. It continued during the trial.

* * *

"Good morning. Today you'll learn that this woman sitting before you possesses a violent nature that few have ever seen. Mr. Webster says she is intelligent. I'm sure she is. And clever. For years she'd been hiding the evil thoughts and feelings inside her head. But when they were turned loose at last, a man lay dead by her hand.

"We'll never be sure how much planning went into his demise. But, plan or not, the result remains: Kenneth Hagen's body was discovered in his own bed that had been set afire. Having been struck, repeatedly on the head, with a heavy object, his bones and teeth were pulverized into mushy splinters. His face was beaten to a bloody pulp beyond recognition. Who wanted that done? Katie did. Who had the opportunity to do it? Katie did.

"The defendant was at the home of Mr. Hagen. She's sworn that throughout their marriage he'd threatened her. She claimed that marriage ended in divorce because of her fears. She can claim whatever she'd like. Talk is cheap. She has produced nothing to show he'd ever taken true action."

He took a break for a sip of water. As he let his eyes drift downward, he shook his head in apparent amazement. He looked up again directing his gaze at the jurors, encouraging them to pay attention to what he said. To believe him.

"It makes me wonder why she was at his home. If she truly felt the fears she'd claimed, would she have gone to that house out in the country? Don't you wonder that, too?

"Further, I believe the divorce hadn't been enough to satisfy Katie. Perhaps getting rid of him permanently consumed her. Not just out of her life through divorce, mind you, but *permanently.* Do you understand the difference? That makes me think she had a plan. You think about that, too."

Several more days were taken up by the prosecution laying groundwork that described Katie as a woman more obsessed with hatred than fear. He called Kenny's co-workers to testify. Some swore Kenny complained that Katie was a nag. He'd never mentioned to them that he had retaliated against her in any way. Beyond that they all felt that Kenny was a good employee. He was on time every day, worked hard and did a good job. Yes, he used bad language, but not around customers, only with the guys that worked with him. He did have a quick temper, but got over it just as quickly. Just a guy's guy.

With little added to the reports on Kenny the prosecution rested their case.

CHAPTER SEVENTY-ONE

Katie's team couldn't quite believe the things she'd told them. Amongst themselves their most curious question was: if Elwood had untied her why didn't she run? Leave the house? With no convincing evidence either way, they adjusted what Katie had told them. They decided to tell the events how *they* felt they happened, and for Katie's benefit. They altered the story to what might be believed by a jury. After all, their goal was to have her found not guilty. The defense told its own interpretation of the facts.

* * *

Susan was the first called to the strand.

"How long have you known the defendant?"

"We attended school together, beginning with second grade. So, we've been best friends for twenty years or more."

"Does she often have bursts of anger?"

"No."

"Can you describe her personality to the jury?"

"I can. She does a good job at whatever needs to be done. She has always been interested in having a family and creating a comfortable home. She's worked hard at it."

"Does she get along with her co-workers? Friends? Family?"

"I didn't work with her, but we talked about her job. In the beginning she was a teacher, and seemed happy with her position. She was animated and often said how much she enjoyed the children and what she did. Besides me, her friends were, for the most part, other teachers. And family? She was an only child, raised by a nanny more than her parents. So there was no family to speak of."

"How about her husband?"

"In the beginning she loved him. And put up with a lot that I'd never put up with myself."

"A lot of what?"

"Well, um, general unacceptable behavior. Yelling at her. Constant complaining. Getting drunk often and physical abuse. Slamming things. Throwing things. Being physically rough with Marley."

"She told you about it?"

"Sometimes, yes."

"And other times?"

"I didn't actually see or hear a lot of it until after she'd divorced him."

"Tell us what happened then."

"He'd call my house because he believed she and Marley were living there with Joe and me. I wouldn't give him any information. He'd blow up at me. Acting like it was my fault. He'd cuss and carry on and swear he'd find her and destroy her. One way or another."

"He told you that?

"More than once. And finally the car chases were enough to terrify her. And when she went to the police they refused to step in on what they called a domestic issue."

And so it went. Susan stayed strong in her support of Katie. But questions from the prosecution planted seeds of doubt in the minds of the jurors: Susan was Katie's best friend. Would she go so far as to commit perjury on her behalf?

Several of Katie's co-workers were called to the stand. Most admitted that Katie didn't offer much about her personal life to them, but seemed pleased with her job and did it well.

After two weeks of trial the closing arguments were due.

* * *

"Ladies and gentlemen. You've heard the story Katie offered you. Now you can see that all arrows point to her. Only her. No one else. Kenny had no other enemies. It had to be Katie. There were too many coincidences. What she told us was made-up. Designed to get her off the hook. Keep her out of jail. Maybe off death row.

"Her only chance of someone backing up her unbelievable story was Elwood. But he didn't want to be involved in this mess. Obviously, he was so embarrassed he's gone into hiding until this ugly ordeal is over.

"Let me remind you of how vicious a crime it was: she hit Kenny in the face with a heavy object, possibly a sledge-hammer, rendering him unconscious. That didn't satisfy her. She continued to wield the weapon with all energy she could supply. Apparently, that was more that enough. Certainly her intent was to leave the body unable to be positively identified, even through dental records. Did she feel a thrill as she smashed his face repeatedly? We'll never know the answer to that. Was she was finally getting even with him? I'd say so: his teeth and jawbone were reduced to mush. Yes, *mush.*

"We all know a sledge-hammer is heavy. But anger can fuel undiscovered strength. Searching for that strength she found it. And, once it surfaced, she spun out of control and couldn't stop until he was pulverized beyond recognition. That, not being sadistic enough to suit her, remember the final insult she delivered: she set fire to the bed he lay in. The very bed they'd once shared as man and wife.

"Surely, she deserves similar punishment. The law won't allow that exactly, but a lethal injection would suffice."

* * *

"We can't deny Katie had motive. She'd been physically and verbally abused for years. Kenny repeatedly suggested, no, threatened, he might kill Katie as well as their young daughter.

"Yes, we freely admit she also had opportunity: his friend, Elwood, called urging her to come to her ex-husband's house. He claimed Kenny was in bad shape, suggested he was quite sick, and needed her help. Elwood knew Katie, after all, was a nice person. A helpful person. She'd moved on with her life and wished the same for Kenny.

"I know you've heard testimony from both sides. Let me re-cap the scenario for you. The events as they unfolded. Try hard to understand her fears. Realize she knew her very life was at stake and she needed to think things through carefully and work out a plan to escape.

"Elwood had promised to stay. He was trustworthy and swore to intervene if Kenny went into one of his tirades or got physical with her. She believed him. Based on that belief she grudgingly agreed to go for a short time.

"Kenny seemed fine when she arrived. Later she felt certain

Elwood lied to please Kenny. The entire plan appeared to be a hoax to get Katie show up. Perhaps even reconcile with Kenny.

"However, Kenny sent Elwood out to buy lunch for the three of them. While he was gone, Katie felt uncomfortable and wanted to leave. Kenny grabbed her as she tried to make her way toward the door.

"Now let me remind you of what happened after that."

Pausing to give time for those first thoughts to establish ground in the minds of the jurors Mr. Webster buttoned one button of his suit jacket and stood still. His hands clasped behind his back, his head down. Then he looked up and watched the faces of the jurors in an attempt to get an idea of how they might be leaning. He paced the floor in front of the table where Katie sat. He returned to face the panel. He took his time to unbutton his jacket again, loosen his tie and began.

"Now listen to this, and listen well. This is the real story of what happened.

"Katie's ex-husband dragged her to the bedroom and choked her with such force she lost consciousness. After tying her to the bed frame he tried to rape her. Failure to perform infuriated him. He became so angry that he choked her again. When Elwood returned with the food Kenny was on top of Katie and she was slowly beginning to regain consciousness.

"Katie overheard the two of them involved in a loud argument because Kenny had promised not to hurt Katie. Elwood defended Katie, infuriating Kenny further. Bordering on violence, they fought. Kenny told Elwood to get out of the house and not to come back. The two men fought again. Elwood finally left when Kenny tried to beat him about the head with a wine bottle.

"As Kenny continued to drink heavily Katie remained tied up. Determined, and working with desperation she finally released the bonds about her wrists. The necktie proved to be the least challenging and came off quickly. Once that had been accomplished her free hand could maneuver the belt buckle. She'd set herself free. Still, she knew she must wait. Timing her escape so as not to be re-captured would require the ultimate patience.

"When Kenny finally flopped down on his bed Katie attempted to judge how close to passing out he was. She'd had years of experience figuring out his level of intoxication. Believing his mind had wandered beyond reality she slipped away, pulled her clothes on and hurried out of the house. When she left Kenny may have had a lit cigarette in his hand. She couldn't be sure.

"She didn't learn of Kenny's death until the police came to arrest her. She'd neither seen nor heard from either of the men since she escaped, and had no idea of Elwood's whereabouts.

"If a sledge-hammer had been used, could Katie possibly have wielded such a heavy tool? Perhaps. But still, after tearing the place apart, police found no such item at the scene or on the grounds.

"There were no witnesses. No one saw her leave or come home. If she'd done what they are trying to make you believe don't you think there'd be blood in her car? On her clothes On her driveway? Well, ladies and gentlemen, none was found in any of those places.

"Why, you ask? Because she did not kill Kenny Hagen. That's powerful information. Factual information. Keep that it mind because now you have to decide her fate."

CHAPTER SEVENTY-TWO

After several grueling days the trial wrapped up. The judge turned responsibility over to the jury. They had a lot to talk about.

Some people find it hard to believe a woman could commit murder. Particularly one as gruesome as this was. Beyond that, in the minds of many, a murderer is not only a man, but is someone who, almost always, is dangerous looking. Often unattractive or showing 'strange' behavior as well. It's not unusual for him to have a past criminal record of some sort. But a woman like Katie? Elegant, college educated, mother and successful business woman? To see her sitting there, listening to a murder charge against her made no sense.

She didn't appear tiny or fragile, but vulnerability seemed to glow around her like a halo. This case would not be a slam-dunk for either side.

As members of the jury listened, for days, to both sides of the argument, the weight of each became heavy. Friends, co-workers, and total strangers all had opinions and seemed eager to share them to anyone willing to listen.. Some by testifying, others in daily conversation among themselves. Yet, none stepped up with negative statements about Kenny that might have helped Katie. Some of the men he'd worked with testified that he'd complained about her nagging. But, surely, that wasn't enough to provoke his alleged threats into action.

And his best friend, Elwood, who Katie said, had heard many of those threats, couldn't be located. His apartment had been abandoned. Rent remained unpaid although notices requesting, then demanding, payment had been sent. Eventually, the manager arranged to have the contents disposed of. No one in the area had heard from him or seen him in the two years since Kenny's death. He had not returned to work. His bank account had been closed shortly after the body had been found. His charge cards had been used only locally for a month or so afterward. Had he gone into hiding? Maybe even left the country?

Katie's co-workers testified little about her fears. Not wanting to be the object of pity or gossip, she'd described them only to her employer when asking that no personal information be given out about her. Susan, of course, proved Katie's best witness. She'd also suffered some verbal abuse from Kenny, especially once he'd suspected Katie and Marley had come to live with her and her husband Joe. She was well aware of Kenny's temper and threats.

CHAPTER SEVENTY-THREE

With every seat in the courtroom filled, people spilled into the hallway hoping to be among the first to hear the verdict. Uniformed men closed the heavy mahogany doors and forced the onlookers to move to the bottom of the marble stairway near the entrance of the building.

"She deserves the death penalty."

"How can you convict her? They don't even know for sure if it's Kenny or not."

"Of course it was Kenny. It was his house."

"Look at her. I don't believe for a minute she did it. Or could do it."

"The remains were unidentifiable."

"Women can do crazy things. I think she did it."

"She's a mother. She wouldn't do something stupid like that to make her abandon her little girl. She'll fight. She's like a lion."

" She's really smart and good at lying and covering it up."

And so it went. The crowd continued to argue back and forth about her guilt or innocence.

* * *

Many lawyers are superstitious about the length of time a jury takes in deliberations. Some seem to believe that when a decision is made quickly the verdict is guilty. If they take longer, you can only come to the conclusion that the jurors are divided and need to work harder at agreeing. After wading through the pros and cons they often acquit.

The foreman signaled they'd reached a verdict. A door to the side of the bench swung open. A bailiff ushered the jury into the courtroom. Someone coughed. A few papers rustled. Then, all movement and noise stopped. The utter and complete silence reeked of doom. The jury had been out three days.

Katie sat at the table, still holding her head high, a box of tissues within easy reach. Mr. Webster rested his arm loosely across the back of Katie's chair. He bent his head toward hers and whispered something. She responded with a weak smile. He patted her shoulder.

The bailiff took the folded slip of paper handed to him and passed it to the judge. The judge opened it, read it silently and returned it to the bailiff to read aloud.

"We the jury, find Katie Hagen…

not guilty of murder in the first degree."

CHAPTER SEVENTY-FOUR

Years flew by in peace. Marley, now eighteen years old and off for college a few days earlier, had blossomed into an intelligent and responsible young lady. Katie, felt very proud of Marley, and satisfied that she'd been a good mom to her. Added to that, being very successful in her job, she thought, that at long last, she'd found the path to sanity.

Friday night. The work-week was over. With no plans made, she could kick back and relax the entire weekend. Maybe she'd give Susan a call and they'd meet for lunch or catch a movie tomorrow night.

As she reached for the phone, it rang. Laughing at the coincidence she picked it up and said "Hello".

"Hiya, Kates, how ya'doin'?"

END

ABOUT THE AUTHOR

Born in Washington, D.C., Sheryl lived most of her life there, or in its suburbs, with the exception of a few years in Whiteville, NC. The daughter of a writer and an artist, Sheryl has worked in oils, acrylics, and several other mediums, the most recent being watercolor. She is also an accomplished photographer. At the age of ten, she published a four-line verse in the *Washington Times Herald* for the payment of one dollar. Since then much of her writing has been non-fiction, directed to trade magazines. Two novels and five children's picture books are now in the works. Flower gardening, inspired by a trip to the butterfly conservatory in Niagara Falls, Canada, is one of her hobbies. Throughout the warm months of the year, her back yard is filled with dozens of varieties of butterflies. Sheryl is animated and has a sense of humor, and as 2003-2004 president of the Ormond Writers' League ran successful meetings with a casual observance to *Robert's Rules of Order*.

Books to date: order on Amazon Books

__Almost Scared to Death__   a true story - 2013

__Katie Did__   *a novel – 2014*